THE

COACH

THE COACH

BY
JOSHUA WALKER

Hardback ISBN 979-8-9936301-0-6
Softback ISBN 979-8-9936301-1-3
E-Book ISBN 979-8-9936301-2-0

First Edition, 2025

Book Cover by 100Covers

For My Players

PART I

THE JOB

CHAPTER 1

For the longest time, Jason Nash didn't have the slightest idea what he wanted to do with his life. He can recall back as far as elementary school, his teachers asking the class, "What do you want to be when you grow up?" His classmates often answered with professions like "firefighter" or "police officer." What always astounded Jason was not the answers they gave, but the certainty with which his fellow classmates gave them. *How can anyone be so sure of what they want to do with their life at such a young age?*

As he sits at his small wooden desk in his tiny one-bedroom apartment, staring past the blank computer screen in front of him to the television behind it, he can't help but let his mind wander back to those days.

Jason had found that growing up with no clue of what you want to do with your life is a surprisingly blissful journey—right up until it isn't. He spent his adolescent and teenage years focusing on building relationships with those around him, creating friendships, and doing anything in his power to bring those friends some happiness, while never really concerning himself with his own. If there was even the smallest chance he could do something that would make a friend smile, he would do it. It was fulfilling to see the people he cared about succeed, but whenever someone would ask him about *his* future, or if *he* needed anything, a pit would form in his stomach—a helpless, sinking feeling, that maybe, deep down, his need to help others was merely a distraction from focusing on himself.

"And there you have it! A buzzer-beater goal to end the half! What an electric way to head into the locker room for the Big Orange!" the overzealous sportscaster yells through Jason's television set, snapping him back to reality. He's watching this week's NCAA lacrosse matchup between his alma mater, Syracuse, and Cornell University. Although the two teams play in different conferences, this is a storied rivalry and always an exciting game to watch. With Syracuse and Cornell heading into their locker rooms, Jason reaches for his remote to mute the TV and wiggles his computer mouse, bringing the screen back to life.

Back to work.

As a twenty-nine-year-old man living in Albany, New York, Jason has spent the last four years coaching at a local high school for their varsity boys lacrosse team.

After college, it had taken him a little while to find coaching as a career, and had it not been for his high school lacrosse coach and current mentor, Chuck Garcia, he may never have. But just as uncertain as he felt back in elementary school when he was asked about his future, the first time Jason stepped onto a lacrosse field as a coach, he knew this was where he was meant to be.

Jason doesn't want to say goodbye to his current job, and more specifically, his current team. He's made real change within this program, and the players genuinely respect and revere him; nevertheless, leaving is something he feels he has to do. Whenever he starts to have his doubts, he can hear Chuck's low baritone voice reverberate throughout his brain: *"Move or rust."* Chuck is always looking out for Jason's future, refusing to let him stagnate—a quality that mildly irritates him at times, though he knows it's what he needs from his mentor.

All of these thoughts are circling around in his head as he opens his inbox, finding three new emails waiting for him to read. The first is spam, a new fitness routine boasting claims to "help you get ripped in two weeks, or your money back." *Ha! Like I need any help with that. I came out of the womb looking like Michelangelo's* David, he thinks, ever the sarcastic narcissist. "Goodbye!" he says aloud as he slams the delete button on his keyboard, causing a puff of dust to shoot out from in between the keys.

The second email is from the Syracuse Alumni Association asking for donations. This email also triggers an auditory response. "Nope!" he proclaims, smashing the delete button on his keyboard a second time. It's not that he doesn't want to support his former school, but he's still in the process of paying back a mountain of student loan debt, and the thought of them asking for even *more* of his money seems unbelievably greedy to him. Finally, he arrives at the third email. It's an email he's received many times since he began his search for a new coaching job three months ago, but it still never gets any easier to read: "Thank you for your interest in the head coaching position at our university. However, we write to inform you that . . ."

He doesn't need to keep reading. These emails all start and end exactly the same way. "Thank you, but fuck you," he mutters to himself angrily, his heart rate increasing as his face goes cold and his mind drifts to a lonely, dark place. Before he lets himself get too far down this rabbit hole of animosity and rage, he snaps himself back to the present by taking a long, deep breath and repeating the phrase, "Never stop, never stop, never stop . . ." Chuck gave him this technique to help quell the dark thoughts when they come knocking on his doorstep—a "Mantra," he called it. It always seemed a bit silly to Jason—that a little phrase can have any effect at all on a person's mental state—but he trusts his mentor implicitly, so he keeps at it. As his heartbeat slows, he goes to delete the message from his inbox, but he hesitates briefly as he sees, and reads aloud, his own email signature: "Think Dan Campbell meets Ted Lasso . . . and there you'll find Jason Nash."

Following Chuck's advice, he includes this signature at the end of every outgoing email he sends to job prospects. A small part of Jason always found it a tad ridiculous comparing himself to a real-life football coach and a fictional soccer coach, but he leaves it in anyway, because oddly enough, he does feel it to be fairly accurate.

Jason closes the laptop; it's only been a few minutes, but he already needs a break. Though he thinks highly of his ability to persevere through adversity, he still can't deny the surge of defeat that washes over him every time he receives a rejection letter.

His gaze shifts over to his apartment's picture window. The golden rays of the setting sun are peeking through the shades as they dance ever so slightly back and forth from the slight breeze coming in. With this breeze comes the welcoming smell of freshly cut grass, reminding him of simpler times, like when he used to run around as a kid with his twin sister, playing games they made up in their backyard. These memories only become more and more vivid as his eyes drift from the window to a photo of the two of them sitting on his desk. He smiles every time he looks at it, their names carved into the mahogany frame with the phrase "Together Forever" engraved on a brass nameplate at its base. The photo was taken on their sixteenth birthday; a large grin is plastered across each of their faces. As he admires it, his fingers press hard into the tattoo of a water lily on his wrist—a habit he formed shortly after entering his freshman year of college, whenever he felt stressed or on edge.

As a wave of emotion crashes down upon him, he knows he can't look at another job posting today in his current mental state—for fear of throwing his laptop through the same glass window that is being so elegantly lit by sunshine at this current point in time—so he slowly lowers his head down onto the cold, hard desk. *If I can have just one brief moment of calm,* he thinks, *I may be able to soldier on.*

Less than thirty seconds later, he hears, "Vrrr, vrrr," the always recognizable sound of his phone vibrating on the flat, rigid surface.

"Ha!" he snorts, shaking his head. "Guess I won't be getting that moment of peace after all."

Seeing that it's Chuck calling, he answers it quickly: "Hey, Chuck."

"What's wrong, Jason?"

"What do you mean, 'what's wrong'?" Jason replies, taken aback by how accusatory the response sounds, even if he's right.

"I mean . . . what's . . . wrong?" Chuck responds, deliberately adding a short pause in between each word, letting the statement sink in. Jason knows when he's been made.

"How'd you know?"

"Jason, you know what the one problem is with you trying to be so positive all the time? When you're in a bad mood . . . it's not hard to tell."

"Shit, am I really that easy to read?" Jason has always been impressed by his mentor's keen ability to read people.

"First off, yes—when people wear their heart on their sleeve, it's easy to tell when something's off. Secondly . . . that's ten push-ups."

"Oh, fuck you," Jason says in a playful, teasing tone.

"That's twenty now, do you want me to keep going?"

Jason rises from his chair, chuckling as he gets down on all fours. For as long as Jason has known him, Chuck has always made any player that swore during practice do ten push-ups, on the spot, no exceptions. He says it helps with discipline.

"I'll count with you, bring the phone to the floor and tell me when you're ready," Chuck adds, matter-of-factly.

"You sure you can count that high, old man?"

"You want me to go to thirty?"

Another smile forms on Jason's face. As he stares down at his hands, shoulder-width apart on the stained, scuffed-up floor, he realizes how much joy this man brings into his life. Just five minutes ago, his best idea for improving his mood was to hurl his expensive laptop through a plate-glass window—and now he's doing push-ups on a dirty wooden floor, and he couldn't be happier.

After completing the twenty push-ups with ease, Jason picks himself up. His knees are a bit red and sore from their short stint being pressed against the floor, but otherwise, he's feeling good.

"Alright, so are you going to tell me what's bothering you now?" Chuck wastes no time returning to the conversation, and Jason admires his no-nonsense way of communicating.

"I just feel stuck . . . you know? I got another rejection letter today, from a school I didn't even want to coach at, but it still sucks. It feels like things aren't coming together for me, and I can't help but . . ." Jason stops to catch his breath, realizing he's been talking so fast, he hasn't had time to breathe. "I can't help but think that I'll never find another school that wants to hire me . . . Am I fooling myself? Am I not good enough?"

A long silence follows. Jason hears nothing but light static on the phone line and the sound of his overhead ceiling fan humming above him. A full ten seconds pass. There's a strange tension in the air before Jason speaks again: "So . . .? Do you have anything you'd like to say back, mentor?"

"I just wanted to let you sit with those words, so you could hear how absolutely ridiculous they sound," Chuck responds.

"Excuse me?"

"Let me ask you something, Jason. How long did it take you to secure your current job, even with my help in setting up interviews and offering myself as a reference?"

"Close to a year." Jason already knows where his mentor is going with this, but he doesn't stop him.

"Exactly. And how long have you been at it with this current job search?"

"No more than three months."

Again, Chuck lets Jason sit with his own words, allowing the full effect of his point to be driven home.

"Has anyone ever told you that you're a smart guy?"

"Not nearly enough, my friend, not nearly enough." There's a slightly facetious tone in Chuck's voice, and though Jason can't actually see him, he's sure there's a grin forming across his face.

They both let out a laugh, appreciating this brief yet friendly exchange. Jason always enjoys it when he gets to see his mentor's softer, fun side.

"So, are you going to keep at it with your job search? Or will this minor lapse in confidence be the straw that broke the camel's back?"

Jason gives a chuckle, mildly amused—he knows a rhetorical question when he hears one. After waiting a beat, he simply replies, "Never stop."

"Never stop," Chuck says. "You've never been a quitter; don't you dare start now. We'll talk soon, my friend. Good luck."

As Jason sets his phone back down on the desk in front of him, his stomach gives a loud *rumble*. It's not uncommon for him to get so caught up in his daily grind that he forgets to eat, sometimes even skipping meals altogether. Remembering there's a full-length Italian sub sitting in his fridge, he makes his way to the kitchen. His mouth begins salivating as he imagines the combination of Italian meats, lettuce, pickles, red onions, and a heavy drizzle of honey mustard dressing. When Jason opens the fridge, he pauses, allowing the cold air to flood out and wash over his face and neck, sending a chill down his spine and making his hair stand on end. These little moments of peace allow him a short escape from the many stressors that have been tugging on his brain as of late.

When he removes the tape from the paper sandwich wrapping, and opens it to reveal the treasure hiding within, the penetrating aroma of capicola is the first to hit his nose and stimulate his senses. As he reaches for the herb and cheese covered bread, he hears that same unmistakable sound coming from the other room: *Vrrr, vrrr.*

Jason drops his head and sighs. "What else could this man want to say to me?"

He then walks back into his bedroom and snatches the phone off his desk, but just as he's about to answer, he stops when he sees the caller ID: *Call From: Unknown Caller.*

Who the hell could this be?

Assuming it's some kind of spam caller or telemarketer, he answers, hoping to give himself a little bit of joy as he messes with whoever is on the other end. Before he has the time to let out a humorous quip, the person on the other end speaks first: "Hello, is this Coach Nash I am speaking with?"

"This is he," Jason responds, slightly confused about who would address him as "Coach Nash." "Who is this?"

"Glad we could connect! My name is Jimmy Buckner of Crystal Summit University. I found your resume online, and I'd love to talk with you about a coaching opportunity within our organization."

CHAPTER 2

Jason sits at his desk, motionless, his eyes staring straight ahead at nothing in particular. His mind is a blur as he recounts the phone call that just took place.

Jimmy Buckner just offered him an assistant coaching position on a women's lacrosse team located just outside of Pittsburgh, Pennsylvania. The recruiter explained that the current head coach of their program, who was currently the only member of the coaching staff, was all alone and in over his head. "Drowning" was the word the recruiter had used.

Assistant coach? Women's lacrosse? Pittsburgh? It all sounds surreal as he recalls every aspect of the job that was just offered to him. *It was offered to him . . . right?* His thoughts are in complete disarray. He looks over the sticky notes in front of him, observing the chicken scratch handwriting scrawled all over them—his penmanship is subpar on a good day, and this is certainly not his best work. As his eyes dart from note to note, they land on one that states, "START DATE - 3 WEEKS." *Okay, so he did offer me the job.* Next to that sticky note lies another one reading, "Needs an answer within 24 hours." Jason's mind gradually comes back into focus as the situation sets in. He was just offered a collegiate coaching job—the thing he'd been searching for—and he was now on the clock to give them an answer. This new reality thrust upon him triggers an entirely different set of emotions to roll over him.

"What the hell do I know about coaching women's lacrosse?" he says aloud, as if accusing himself of being underqualified—or just straight up *unqualified.* "And an assistant coach . . .? Seems like a step backward . . ."

Before continuing with this barrage of self-ridicule, he stops himself—he has been told more than once that when a big, life-changing opportunity presents itself, he has a tendency to spiral and talk himself out of it. *"Avoiding change out of fear,"* he remembers an old high school teacher calling it.

In an effort to stop the spiral, he quickly reaches into his desk drawer and grabs a sheet of plain white paper. At the top, he writes, "Pros and Cons," and then draws a line down the center of the paper, stopping momentarily at the bottom of the page after noticing his hand is shaking rather intensely. He balls his fist a few times, flexing his fingers and making his forearm pulsate—an exercise that, in the past, has helped stave off the shaky, anxious feeling that is slowly creeping up inside him. He gives his head a quick shake and blinks a few times to bring his mind back to the present. Jason has always found a pros and cons list to help when facing a decision that has provoked thoughts of uncertainty, and he's hoping it'll help now as well.

On the "pros" side he writes, "New opportunity, college job, better pay." Unable to think of anything else, he moves his attention to the "cons" side of the paper. Without thinking, he starts to write. When he's done, he observes the words scribbled on the page: "Assistant coach—feels like a step backward. Women's lacrosse—never coached it. New city—scary." He places his pen down on the desk and looks over the list—three pros and three cons. *Great,* he thinks, *not helpful.*

Jason's mind is still a mess. He considers calling Chuck back to get his advice, but he's feeling vulnerable, and if he's being honest with himself, a little scared too. This isn't necessarily a bad thing, but he knows Chuck will want to dig into those feelings, and right now, that's the last thing Jason wants to do. *If I wanted to talk about my feelings, I'd call a shrink,* he thinks, only partly joking, but fully aware that it's probably exactly what he needs.

Chuck has suggested therapy to Jason on more than one occasion, reassuring him that it might help in coping with the challenging emotions he sometimes struggles with. Fear, doubt, insecurity, anger—these are all things that aren't great to hold on to, especially when you're coaching and mentoring young athletes.

"You should talk to someone, Jason," he would insist. But Jason always deflected by saying something snarky: *"Why would I need to talk to someone else about my feelings? I talk to myself in the mirror every morning! And he only sometimes talks back."* He would always add a wink at the end to emphasize the sarcasm in his response. Chuck would just shake his head and give a disapproving sigh, knowing Jason was too stubborn to relent. This always left Jason in a somewhat somber mood. He didn't like the idea of his mentor being disappointed in him, but he also didn't feel the need to change.

Realizing the pros and cons list hasn't helped, he sits back in his desk chair and stares directly upward, observing every crack in his wooden ceiling; he notices a small dent in one of the cross-beams from the time he opened a bottle of champagne a bit too excitedly one night. The cork had shot out of the bottle with a loud *"pop"* and left its mark—too high up for Jason to fix, not that he really cared all that much. He thinks back to that night: *Why had I been celebrating?* After some recollection, it came to him. That was the day Chuck had called Jason to inform him that he had been offered the high school coaching job where he currently works—beating out three other candidates for the position.

Thinking back, he remembers every little detail of that phone call. The giddiness that rapidly flowed through his body when he heard the news. The goosebumps that covered his arms and wouldn't go away. He felt weightless, filled with pure, unwavering happiness as an enormous smile formed across his face.

His life changed in a big way that day. He threw caution to the wind and leaped into the great unknown of whatever came next. Taking on a new challenge in coaching hadn't scared him then, so he wasn't about to let it scare him now. As his mind comes careening back to the present, he sits upright in his chair, with a look of determination in his eyes, while he levels his gaze and reaches for his phone.

"Fuck it," he says aloud, just before hitting "redial"—his words carrying a sense of purpose and ambition, without even the slightest hint of impulsivity or fear.

CHAPTER 3

As Jason sits in a smooth, powder blue chair located in the large Pittsburgh field house—the cold leather of the chair offering some comfort as it presses against his skin on this humid spring morning—he does his best to appear patient as he waits to meet with his new athletic director. Jason is scheduled to take a tour of the facilities with him and the head coach this morning, to get a "lay of the land" is how the AD had put it in the email he received a few days ago.

The previous three weeks had been an absolute haze. After finishing up the call with the recruiter—the very reason he's now sitting in this comfortable chair—he had gotten straight to work.

Packing up his apartment to prepare for the move wasn't too much of a challenge. Jason has never been one to get too attached to material things, and truthfully, he doesn't own that much to begin with. His sparse one-bedroom only took two days to fully clean out, and then it was just a matter of relocating what little he owns into the new housing provided by the university, and doing his best to get settled in.

Uprooting his entire life and moving nearly seven hours to a place he'd never even visited—nor knew anything about—seemed rather daunting at first. But Jason prides himself on his ability to compartmentalize his emotions, especially when things get overwhelming. He's always found that if he doesn't allow his mind to stop thinking, or his body to stop moving, and focuses only on the next task at hand, it's an efficient way to get through chaotic times.

The problem with this, however, is that once you take a minute to stop and process what's happening, the weight of all the massive change you've just gone through quickly comes crashing down, and the feeling of angst and unease can take over. This reality is becoming more and more prevalent in his current situation as Jason notices his right leg bouncing rapidly up and down in the chair, his breathing matching this tumultuous rhythm, while his eyes dart around the room, landing on nothing in particular. Amidst his mind racing, a thought forms in his head—a thought he'd locked away, but somehow, it found its way out. *Did I make a colossal mistake coming here?*

Before he has time to contemplate this question, the door to the athletic director's office swings open, disturbing the silence in the room.

"Jason Nash, I presume!" he states emphatically, extending his right arm for a handshake. "The name's Bill, Bill Chapman. So nice to finally meet you."

"Yes, that's me," Jason replies as he grips the large, firm hand in front of him, hoping his hand isn't at all clammy from the small, frantic episode that just took place.

"I hope the wait wasn't too long. I was just finishing up a call with your new head coach, Jim Dickerson," Bill replies, and Jason notices something slightly strange with the tone of his voice, but he just brushes it aside.

"Oh, that's great. I'm really looking forward to meeting him. When will he be joining us on the tour?"

"Well . . . he won't be, unfortunately. He's a little under the weather, so he's taking the day off. But he'll be at your first practice tomorrow, and he said he's already got everything planned, so don't you worry."

The feeling of unease creeps effortlessly back into Jason's mind. "Are you sure he'll be okay for tomorrow?" Jason can hear the hint of worry in his own voice—he's a confident man, but the thought of having no guidance in a new position, on the first day, doesn't bring him much comfort.

"Yes, yes. Absolutely. He'll be here," Bill replies reassuringly. "Now, let's begin your tour. I cannot wait to show you everything this wonderful facility has to offer."

Jason pushes past any latent feelings of uncertainty as the two set off. He can hear Chuck's words echoing throughout his mind: *Don't worry until you have something to worry about.* This was another piece of advice he gave him often, reminding him that there's no reason to give yourself undue stress from worry if you aren't certain of the future that lies ahead of you.

As Jason walks side by side with his new boss, listening closely as he describes everything they walk by in great detail—a speech that he's sure the man has given a thousand times—he's amazed at how vast and beautiful everything around him appears. There are crystal clear glass display cases, enshrining tall bronze trophies from championships won in years past. The pristine white walls are covered in banners and lined with powder blue edging and accents. Even the way it smells as they walk through the halls catches Jason off guard; he is used to the stale, somewhat pungent, smell of sweat and dirt that would emanate from the locker rooms at his previous high school job. But this place smells crisp and clean—almost radiant and uplifting, as if teeming with potential. *Guess that's what university money gets you,* he thinks, smiling, but then something else pops into his head.

"Something wrong?" Bill asks, interrupting his thoughts.

"No, it's just that . . . I just realized I have no idea what our mascot is here."

Even as the words come out of his mouth, Jason recognizes how unprofessional it must sound that he doesn't know this trivial yet important detail of the job he's just accepted. Thankfully, Bill doesn't seem to show any concern about his response.

"We're the Blue Jays!" he replies, beaming with pride, which brings Jason some relief. *Good, at least this guy has some passion for his school.*

"Incredible!" Jason says, trying his best to match Bill's energy.

Even as Jason replies, he quietly considers that a blue jay isn't the most intimidating of mascots. *A bird?* he thinks, recalling the menacing cougar mascot of his former team.

The tour continues throughout the mazelike field house, with every turn offering new and intriguing sights for Jason to take in. Rounding one final corner, Bill brings them to a long hallway that appears to stretch for miles, leading to a set of large double doors at the end. Down the hallway, about every ten feet, there's a single spotlight on each side, facing downward toward a banner hanging beneath it. The spacing of the lights offers a strange, almost ominous lighting scheme as they walk.

"Wow . . ." The word slips out of Jason's mouth without warning as he stares down the never-ending chasm.

"I know. Amazing, isn't it? This is the hallway that leads to our lacrosse field. On game day, both teams have to walk this long stretch of carpet before taking the field together."

Jason just stands there, taking in the magnitude of the sight in front of them.

"The official name given to this hallway is *The Tunnel of Champions*, but I have always referred to it as *The March to Hell*, because it reminds every opponent exactly what they're in for when they take the field—a battle of unbridled proportions and a challenge comparable only to walking through the gates of hell themself."

A chill shoots down Jason's spine. He has always considered himself a motivational speaker—his former team often giving him props on how his pregame speeches would inspire them to fight harder—and after hearing what Bill has just said, he can't help but admire the man. *Passionate, motivational, and also harboring some semblance of a dark side . . . I like this guy.*

Jason's eyes move from banner to banner as he makes his way down the hall with Bill. Each one is roughly four feet long, black with bright blue and white letters, and contains the year in which the lacrosse team had won a championship in the past. While Jason observes the multitude of championships this program has won, something else comes to mind. He hesitates briefly but speaks up anyway. "Can I ask you a question?"

"Yes, of course. What's on your mind?"

"Well . . . I don't want to sound like I don't think I'm worthy of this job . . . But, sir, I was a high school boys lacrosse coach. I have never coached women's lacrosse. And seeing all these banners of achievement . . . it makes me wonder why the current coach *needed* any help, and also, why you chose me."

Before Bill answers, he stops walking. They are nearly at the end of the hallway, about five feet from the double doors that lead out to the field.

"Jason, to answer your first question, look around us now and tell me what you see." He gestures to the walls around them.

As Jason's eyes survey their surrounding area, he notices there's nothing hanging around them. There are no more banners, just evenly spaced spotlights illuminating bare, white walls.

"We won our last championship over a decade ago, and we haven't had a winning season in five years," Bill says flatly. "The team is in shambles, and it's in desperate need of a culture change. They are sick of losing, and they choose to take out their frustration and insecurities on each other instead of accepting responsibility and moving forward. Don't get me wrong; our current head coach is a tactile mastermind, but he lacks the ability to relate with these women, and without a change, I just don't know if he'll ever get us back on track."

Jason takes a full ten seconds to process this information. This is a new side of Bill he hasn't seen yet, a side of him that lacks all humor and levity, and he appears determined yet worried, all at the same time.

"Okay . . . So, the coach *does* need help," Jason replies. "But why—"

"Why did I choose you?" Bill says abruptly, as if reading Jason's mind. "Because of this."

Reaching into his pocket, Bill pulls out his cell phone, opens up a video, and clicks "play." Jason is shocked as he sees himself on the phone screen, surrounded by his old team in the pouring rain, screaming as loud as he can:

> Alright, men, listen up! I know we've been watching the weather all day, waiting to see if a storm was coming. Well . . . a storm has come, but this isn't a storm that rains down from the heavens. This is a storm that showed up on this field an hour ago, and now stands before me, ready to *fight*! So, to my offense, I ask that when you walk out there today, you strike down like lightning and set that field ablaze!
>
> And defense, I want your thunderous voices to echo throughout time! This is where we triumph; this is where we conquer. This is where we win, and this is where they lose!

As the players that surround Jason on the screen proceed to jump up and down like wild animals, and the sound of thirty screaming lacrosse players roars out from the phone's speaker, Bill pauses the video and looks up at Jason.

"My son showed me this video about a month ago. He said it popped up on his Instagram Reels as he was scrolling from video to video."

"I don't understand . . . You hired me because of what I said in this video?"

"No. I hired you because of how your team responded. As I watched that video, I saw thirty or so players who were willing to fight and die for you. They were willing to walk through the gates of hell for you. It isn't that they *had* to follow you; it was that they *wanted* to follow you."

Again, Jason is stunned by Bill's words. He was simply leading his team in the best way he knew how. He hadn't known that someone was recording him.

"Jason, listen, I know this is all a lot to take in. You're in a new place, starting a new job, surrounded by people and things you do not know—but take a look back down this tunnel we just walked through."

They both turn and gaze back down the seemingly endless hallway.

"These banners are for people who live in the past. They commemorate a bygone era, showing nothing more than what this program once was. I am looking for someone to help take this program into the future, and I believe that person is you."

After Bill finishes speaking, he turns back around and pushes through the double doors that now stand in front of them at the end of the hall. Jason lifts his left arm to shield his eyes as a massive wave of light floods in. It takes a minute for his eyes to adjust, but when they do, he realizes they're standing just outside of the lacrosse field. The world becomes still. His eyes scan all around him as he admires the large, metallic bleacher seating that stretches high into the sky.

He bends down and brushes his hand over the bright green turf, feeling the faint heat radiating from below. As he stands back up, taking a deep breath, the stress dissipates from his body. *What the hell was I so worried about?* he thinks, feeling almost foolish, as he continues to take in all the wonders of the stadium. Jason remains in this reveling trance until Bill speaks again.

"So . . . big day tomorrow. First day of collegiate coaching, first day of practice, and . . . you get to meet the team."

CHAPTER 4

As they approach the locker room, Jason isn't sure what to expect. He couldn't sleep last night in anticipation of meeting the team. He can recall meeting his previous high school team like it was yesterday, remembering how there was a strange balance of skepticism and apathy in the air. Most people aren't the biggest fans of change, so this wasn't a big surprise to him at the time, and he knew he'd get the opportunity to win them over. These same feelings are flowing through Jason as he nears the locker room. He can hear the sound of women's voices emanating from behind the door. A rush goes through his body, realizing this is the first time he's actually felt truly excited over the last few weeks.

Jason experienced many emotions leading up to today—happiness, worry, anxiety, and even confusion—but this feeling of excitement as he walks toward the locker room is one that causes him to smile uncontrollably. *This is what it's all about,* he thinks, as the sounds emitting from the locker room slowly get louder, then pause, before laughter erupts from behind the door. Jason has always appreciated the camaraderie a team shares above anything else—it's like being a part of a second family—something people who don't play sports could never truly understand.

When they enter the locker room, the team goes quiet. There are twenty-two pairs of unblinking eyes staring directly back at Jason, and he knows each and every one of them is trying to figure him out. Bill gives him a quick introduction: "Good afternoon, ladies. This is Jason Nash, your new assistant coach."

Afterwards, he ducks out of the room, leaving Jason all alone—and although he's technically their new leader, he feels more like a minnow that's been tossed into a shark tank.

The silence is deafening, and just as Jason goes to open his mouth, one of the girls stands up to speak. She is tall, close to six feet, with long blonde hair tied up in a large braid. Her tan skin is oddly complementary to the powder blue pinnie she is wearing. Jason also notices a large "C" sewn into the pinnie. *Okay, so she's a captain,* he thinks. *She'll get the ball rolling.* Jason has always appreciated a strong leader as a captain, someone who isn't afraid to stand up and take charge, someone who says what needs to be said, even if it isn't the most popular opinion. For her to stand up so quickly to speak, he takes this as a sign of strong leadership, and a wave of relief rolls over him.

This wave of relief lasts about three seconds, until she says, "Hey, I'm Sam. I've got a question . . . Who the hell do you think you are coming here to coach us?"

Jason is taken aback. He had predicted numerous possibilities for how this conversation might go, but hostile was not one of them. Caught off guard, he hesitates to speak, but then another player jumps in.

"Sam!" she yells, shaking her head in disapproval at her fellow teammate's outburst. "Sorry, Coach. First off, I'm Jenny; nice to meet you. I think what Sam meant to say was—"

"What I *meant* to say," Sam interrupts, "was that I read up on you. A high school boys lacrosse coach with *zero* experience coaching women. You can't teach us anything."

The words just sit there, floating through the air, in a moment that appears to freeze in time. In one sentence, she had validated all of Jason's own concerns regarding his appointment to this job, and simultaneously broken any confidence he'd built up over the last few weeks.

Sam finishes Jason off with one last comment before storming out of the room: "You're not my coach, and you'll never be my coach."

As she exits, the door *slams* behind her, startling the other players. Jason takes a second to compose himself—his heart is beating loudly in his chest, and his blood is pumping at an alarming rate, one that a doctor would most likely call "dangerous."

"Okay, moving on," is all he can muster, his voice wavering ever so slightly. This player has struck a nerve with him, and he's hoping no one in the room can tell.

"I'm sorry about her," Jenny says calmly. "She is not having a great week, and, like everyone here, she's just tired of losing."

"Amen to that," another girl responds, followed by a few more nods of agreement.

Jason can tell there's a lot of emotion running through this team, and he doesn't want to exacerbate it anymore, so he carries on cautiously.

"Listen, in a way, Sam is right. I have no experience in this realm. I have four years of coaching experience, all of which were for a high school boys lacrosse team. As of right now, I don't know anything about you, and you don't know anything about me, but I do know that we share one thing in common." He pauses briefly to survey the room and build some suspense in the air. Seeing he has their attention, he presses on. "We both want what is best for this team, and we both want to win."

After receiving some approving nods from the players and thinking he may have made a sliver of progress, a shorter girl who was sitting near Sam, sporting dark black hair and pale skin covered in freckles, speaks up, "Hey, buddy . . . you just got here."

Before Jason has time to respond, another girl, who looks identical to the one who just spoke, pipes in with a snide remark: "Yeah, how the hell can you say you want what's best for us. You literally *just* met us."

Jason's mind races as he considers a response while also registering that these two girls must be sisters, possibly twins, with the resemblance they bear to each other. Hoping to avoid any more animosity and possibly dodge the blatantly disruptive question, he replies in a leveled tone: "And who might you two be? Twins, I presume?"

"Yeah, my name is None-Ya, and this is my sister, Damn Business. So, I guess you could say our names are None-Ya Damn Business."

Jason takes a deep breath and exhales. *Guess I won't be avoiding that animosity.* Jenny comes to his defense again, interrupting his train of thought.

"Maddy! Nicole! Would you two show at least a shred of respect to our new coach?"

"Ha! *Coach* . . . What a joke," Maddy replies coldly.

This statement strikes a nerve, and before Jenny can chime back in, Jason interrupts. "Enough!"

The room goes dead silent, and many players recoil at the outburst, clearly caught off guard. He doesn't like it when his anger takes over, even in small doses, but he refuses to tolerate such blatant disrespect from his players.

"I can see that, for some of you, my presence here may be unwanted, but alas, I'm not going anywhere. If you have any concerns about me, we can discuss this at a later date. For now, we have about an hour until practice, so get ready, and I'll see you out there."

Before anyone has a chance to say anything back, Jason stands up swiftly and exits, leaving his final words hanging in the air for the entire team to take in.

As he leaves the locker room, his heart rate is still very elevated, and before he even realizes it, he's dialed Chuck's number, and the phone is ringing.

Chuck answers the phone and speaks before Jason can even say hello. "Jason, it's 9 a.m. on your first day. Why are you already calling me?"

Straight to the point as always.

"I just met the team."

"Okay, and how'd it go?"

"Remind me, Chuck, what was that movie starring Leonardo DiCaprio, set in the early nineteen hundreds, about a large boat that sank?"

"Jason, are you really comparing your first meeting with the team to a catastrophe that killed almost fifteen hundred people?"

"I know, I know . . . It's just, it didn't go well, okay?"

"Jason, I'm going to need more information than *'it didn't go well'* if you want me to be of any help."

"Well, where do I begin?" Jason says. "They don't want me here. They don't respect me, and one of them insulted me and then just walked out." Realizing his breathing is fast and uncontrolled, he stops to take a breath.

"Well, it sounds like everything's terrible, and you should just quit, then . . . right? Is that what I'm hearing?" Chuck's response leaves Jason rattled.

"Are you mocking me now?"

"No, Jason. I'm reminding you that every small setback is not a reason to spiral. I'm simply using a hint of sarcasm that you might understand."

Knowing he's right once again, Jason lets out a quick but loud sigh before responding. "Okay, I agree. You're right. I'm not going anywhere. Ironically, I actually used those exact words to the team only moments ago."

"Wait, you actually used the phrase *I'm not going anywhere*? In what context did that come up?"

"Well, one of them sort of scoffed at the mere notion of me being their coach, and then she called me a joke. So, I got a bit defensive. Was that wrong?"

Chuck responds in a cold, flat tone: "Absolutely not. But—"

"There's always a '*but*' . . ." Jason says, interrupting.

"Listen, Jason. Yes, disrespect must be dealt with swiftly, but you also need to understand that these are players in their twenties, and there may be other things going on in their lives that you know nothing about. All I'm saying is, you just met them, and their poor behavior most likely isn't about you. You're just the newest punching bag to unload on."

Jason closes his eyes momentarily, letting the advice sink in. "Okay, so what should I do?"

"Well, how did you win over the players on your high school team?"

"I don't know . . . I was just myself. I opened up about my time as a lacrosse player. I showed off some stick skills, and I even snuck in some clips from an old highlight reel of mine at our first film session." Jason smiles as he remembers how his old players reacted when they saw him score "behind the back" during that film session. "But, Chuck, I have no experience in the realm of women's lacrosse. How can I relate?"

"Well, Jason, we both know that's not true. You *do* have experience in this realm. But moving past the concept of women's lacrosse, you know there are other ways to relate to people, right? There are other ways to open up."

"Yeah, I know, I just—"

"I get it, Jason. Letting people in can be hard, so if you don't feel like opening up, just remember it's still your first day. Also, you're just the assistant, so you'll have help."

This does bring Jason some relief. In all the commotion, he had forgotten he'd have the head coach to steer the ship and assuredly offer some help if any more disrespect came his way.

"And worst-case scenario, just make them run," Chuck adds, in a slightly sarcastic but also serious manner. "There's nothing like a full field sprint to make anyone question whether or not his/her disrespectful comment was worth it."

"Ha!" Jason can't help but laugh as he remembers every time his own words got him into trouble back when he played. "Thank you, Chuck, I don't know what I was so worried about."

"Jason, worrying just means you care, and there's nothing wrong with that. Enjoy your first day."

With that, Chuck hangs up, and Jason proceeds down *The March to Hell* before opening the double doors to the field, again being greeted by a radiant flash of sunshine. *Everything's going to be okay,* he thinks. *Everything's going to be okay.*

CHAPTER 5

No, everything was not okay.

As Jason waited on the field for the team to enter, his eyes kept drifting down to his watch. The head coach had not shown up yet, and every second that passed, while he sat alone on the cold silver bench, made his stomach sink a little further. After three unanswered calls to Bill and seven unanswered text messages, Jason's eyes shift to the gate that stands at the opposite side of the field leading to the parking lot. His mind wanders in a moment of weakness as he imagines how easy it would be to leave this field, get in his car, and never look back.

"No," he says aloud, to no one but himself. "You don't walk away."

Slam!

His one-person conversation is interrupted by the sound of the double doors flying open as the players filter onto the field. He can hear the sound of indistinct chatter as they walk toward him. Jason isn't exactly sure what he wants to say when they get to him, so he leads off with a generic greeting: "Hello again."

"Where's Coach?" Sam replies, completely brushing past his introduction.

"I'm right here."

Sam doesn't hesitate in firing back a response: "I already told you, you're not my coach, an—"

"And I'll never be your coach. I know, I know. I remember what you said," Jason replies. Sam stops short and looks around at her teammates, searching for an answer that no one can give. "Ladies, full disclosure, I have no clue where Coach Dickerson is, but I assure you, when I do, you'll be the first to know. For now, let's just get started—everyone take a quick lap, and we'll go from there."

For a few seconds, no one moves, but then, a wave of acceptance seems to fall over the team as they shrug and take off around the field. *Phew, well, that was painless.*

"Jenny!" Jason calls out. "You stay here. I want to have a quick chat."

As Jenny approaches, there is a hint of apprehension in her eyes, but she greets him calmly and with confidence, nonetheless. "Yeah, Coach, what's up?"

"You seem to be my only real supporter right now, or at least you're the only one who isn't overtly against me being here. So, with that in mind, I was hoping you'd give me a quick rundown of the team."

"Sure thing. Where would you like me to begin?"

"Well, why don't we start with that wonderful bundle of joy, Sam, over there."

Jenny's lips form a quick smile before she wipes it off her face and responds, "Sam is a tremendous defensive player and a true asset to this team, but she can be kind of . . . difficult at times."

"Difficult, eh?" Jason replies with a smirk. "Well, isn't that the understatement of the year."

"She means well—she really does—but her negativity has certainly been a drag, and what's worse is that she truly is a strong leader, so when she gets negative, that attitude tends to spread."

"Fair enough, and speaking of negativity, what can you tell me about the twins? Maddy and Nicole, I think I remember you calling them."

"Ah yes, Maddy and Nicole Shay, or *The Shady Sisters*, as we like to call them. Well, again, they are phenomenal lacrosse players, possibly the best on the team—especially considering it can sometimes appear like they have the ability to read each other's mind on the field, if you can believe that." Jenny chuckles as the words come out of her mouth, as if the idea of telepathy between the two is crazy, but Jason stares back at her with a look of understanding.

"Truthfully, Jenny," he replies, "I can believe it."

Confusion crosses her face, but she continues, "Yes, so, they're great and all, but Sam's really taken them under her wing this year, which means they've now adopted that *wonderful* attitude of hers . . ."

Great, well, at least I know which domino needs to fall first.

"Okay, now, what abou—"

Before he can finish, the team returns from their lap, and they circle up around him. All is quiet except for the sound of their loud, exhaustive breathing.

Jason goes to speak, but he's cut short by a voice that is becoming all too familiar to him. "So, what now, huh? What's the all-knowing women's lacrosse coach got planned for us?" Sam's response is riddled with condescension, *but that's nothing new.*

"Well, Sam, I think we'll start out with some shuttles . . . If that's okay with you, Captain?" Jason immediately realizes he's matched her condescending tone, and he makes a mental note to try and dial it back.

"How . . . do you know what shuttles are?"

"Because, Sam, I'm—oh, how did you put it?—the 'all-knowing women's lacrosse coach.' Would you like me to explain how shuttles work to you?"

More condescension . . . shit. Well, I tried.

Her face grows red as she fumes, but before she can respond, Jenny jumps in, "Alright, ladies, you heard him! Three shuttle lines, seven people per line. Let's get to it."

The next ninety minutes are like a hallucination. Jason is pulling his phone from his pocket every few minutes to check for a text regarding his head coach, like a nervous tick he can't shake. After every drill he has the girls do—most of which are drills he picked up from boy's lacrosse—he can feel the tension rising. His mind is all over the place, and he isn't doing a great job of hiding it. His body feels limp, and his head fuzzy, like a fever dream he can't awaken from. Between every drill, Jason can hear the players whispering amongst themselves, and he can make out subtle fragments of what is being said.

"I don't get it . . ."

"Where's our head coach?"

"What's going on?"

Most of them are harmless, but then he hears one that really piques his interest.

"Who is this guy?"

Jason is reminded of his conversation with Chuck. *"You know there are other ways to relate to people, right?"*

Jason ponders the idea. *Maybe he's right. Maybe I do need to find a way to open up.*

Sam's voice cuts through his thoughts and brings his mind plummeting back to the present. "Hey, *dude*, what's next on your stellar practice plan? And where the hell is our coach?"

"As I have said already, when I hear anything regarding Coach Dickerson, you'll be the first to know," Jason replies. "And please don't call me *dude*."

"Okay, *bro*. What's next?"

Sam makes no effort to hide her disrespect toward him. Jason takes a long, deep breath to calm himself.

"I'd prefer you not use *bro*, either. *Coach* or *Nash* will suffice, if you don't mind."

"How about . . . *bitch*? Does that work for you?"

Jason's face goes cold, and his eyes narrow. There is silence on the field as everyone and everything goes quiet. Jason's eyes remain locked with Sam's, and the entire world around them seems to freeze in this flash of icy indifference. Then suddenly, a lone thought comes into focus in his mind. *What was it that Chuck said?*

"Worst-case scenario, just make them run."

"Alright. Everyone on the end line . . . now."

Sam quickly responds, "Excuse me? Why?"

"This isn't a debate, Sam. Everyone on the end line now." Jason pauses before adding, "But, Sam, I think you know where I'm going with this."

"Okay, everyone, wait." Sam is still commanding as she looks to address the team, but Jason can sense a hint of contrition. "I messed up. I'll do the running. Everyone else, go get some water."

The other players breathe sighs of relief until Jason stops them short.

"Nope."

"What do you mean, *nope*?" Sam asks.

"I said, *everyone* on the end line, and I did not misspeak."

"But . . ."

"Everyone!"

The team relents. First, Jenny walks over, followed by a few more, then the rest follow suit. Jason can hear them quibbling amongst themselves as they do.

"Unbelievable."

"Sam . . . She just had to open her mouth."

"This is bullshit."

As they approach the end line, Jason waits a beat before addressing the team. "Alright, this is going to be very simple. Every time I blow this whistle, you run to the fifty-yard line and back. Got it?"

The players nod half-heartedly, and then he begins.

Fweet!

He blows the whistle, and they take off.

After every turn, running down and back, Jason gives them a short rest before they go again, in a cycle that he is certain feels like hell, but he can only imagine it's the worst for Sam. He remembers all too well what it's like to be in her shoes. The cycle continues for about ten minutes, although to the team, it must feel like hours. Jason has them stop after about fifteen or so sprints. He's lost count himself.

"Listen up!" Jason yells out, his voice already hoarse and his vocal cords strained. "I know this is my first day. I know you don't know me, and I know I'm just *the assistant* . . . But make no mistake, I am here to make a difference."

Most of the team is still keeled over, hands on their knees, desperately trying to catch their breath, but they are listening. He can feel it; he has their attention.

"If you have a problem with any of my methods, let me know, and I will gladly hear you out. But I will not tolerate disrespect." Jason can see some players choosing to nod in agreement, though he's fairly certain they're only doing so because they want the running to stop. *No matter,* he thinks, then presses on. "Over this season, it is my intention to get to know you all, to figure out what makes you tick, and in doing so, give myself the best chance to help you succeed and grow . . . But that doesn't mean I need to be your friend. Do I make myself clear?"

Unsurprisingly, Jenny is the first to respond. "Yes, Coach."

Her response is echoed by most.

"Okay, then, we're done for today; bring it in."

Jason waits as they all filter around him, still winded from the running. They look unhappy, but that's not a shock.

"Ladies, tomorrow, we do not have practice, so I'd ask you to take the day to reflect on how today went." Jason notices a few players roll their eyes in discontent, but he forges on. "If you need anything, let me know, and I will see you all on Monday."

Normally, he'd ask if the team had any questions, but he has a sneaking suspicion that would go off the rails real quick, so instead he locks eyes with Jenny. "Captain, break 'em down."

Jenny walks into the center of the circle as Jason exits. As he walks away, toward the bench, he can hear her shout behind him: "Alright, ladies, sticks up. Jays on three—one, two, three, Jays!"

Hearing the loud roar of their cheer brings a smile to Jason's face, knowing their spirit wasn't totally crushed from the events of the day. As he goes to sit on the bench, his knees give way, and he collapses onto the cold steel. This is followed by a long, deep exhale that allows every ounce of air in his lungs to escape, to release all the chaos and negativity from the day. He is worn out; the weight of the day's stress sits heavily on his shoulders. While he does his best to maintain a look of composure, the team walks past him on their way back through the double doors into the facility. Three of the twenty-two players walk up to acknowledge him.

Jenny approaches him first. "Thanks, Coach. Not ideal, but it'll get better." Jason acknowledges her with a defeated grin, realizing she's currently being way more positive than he is.

The other two players simply say, "Thanks, Coach," before heading inside—he wants to ask their names and have a proper introduction, but his resolve is wearing thin.

Jason remains sitting on the bench as the last player exits the field and the doors close behind her, and he recounts the events of the practice out loud to himself. "Alright, Jason, prioritize the wins . . . First, you had three players say thank you to end the day; it's not much, but it's a start. What is it Chuck likes to say? 'Brick by brick.'"

Jason's eyes have a shimmer as he thinks about his mentor. This passes quickly, however, as he realizes he cannot recall any other "wins" for the day. *No matter,* he thinks. *Brick by brick, right?*

It was a shitstorm of a day, but Jason is relieved at the thought of having tomorrow off to regroup, meet the head coach, *hopefully,* and just relax and prepare for Monday. These moments of bliss are Jason's happy place—the times where he catches himself smiling for no reason at all, except for the simple fact that he feels content in a brief snapshot of stresslessness, on an otherwise stress-ridden day.

Vrr, vrr. His phone suddenly vibrates in his pocket, jolting him out of his happy place. "Probably just good ol' Chuck checking in," he says to himself, retrieving the phone from his pocket. When he looks down at the caller ID, he sees a different name: *Bill Chapman.*

"What incredible timing this guy has," Jason begrudgingly says before answering. "Hey, Bill, nice of you to call me back."

His tone is resentful and riddled with sarcasm in a not-so-subtle manner—which may not be the ideal way to address his boss on the first day—but this was no picnic of a first day.

"Jason, I have some bad news . . . Jim, your head coach, he just quit . . ."

Bill keeps on speaking, but the words trail off as Jason's mind leaves the conversation. His ears start ringing as his vision blurs, and the feeling of nausea floods his body. His arms tremble and go numb, causing the phone to fall from his grip, landing with a loud *thud* on the bench below, all at once snapping Jason back to reality.

He looks down at the phone. "Jason? Jason? Are you there?" He can hear Bill's faint voice coming from the small phone speaker at his side, but he can't seem to pick it back up. He just sits there, staring down at the phone calling his name. After a few seconds, his mind shifts gears, going from a blank slate to a racing nightmare. *Why is this happening to me? Why does everything go south right when it starts to seem okay? Why can't I ever just have one moment of goddamn happiness?!*

The air is still and silent around him, but inside his head, the atmosphere is anything but. His whole body is trembling now, and just as he sees the phone line go dead, he bends at the waist, placing his face into cupped hands. From there, he slowly but aggressively runs his fingers past his face and back through his greasy hair, the veins in his forehead feeling like the roots of a giant sequoia. Every emotion in his body—contempt, sadness, fear, doubt—feels like it's boiling up inside him and transforming into one common feeling of pure, unbridled rage. He rises from the bench in one quick motion, and screams out for no one to hear:

"FUCK!"

CHAPTER 6

Jason is seated across from Bill in his office, the fluorescent lights reflecting off his skin as sweat drips from every pore. He is doing his best to control the shaking that hasn't stopped since he left the lacrosse field. As he sits there restlessly, he realizes he can't remember how he got here. One minute he was standing alone on the field screaming profanity at the heavens above, and the next he's sitting here in the AD's office.

"Listen, Jason. I know this isn't an ideal situation, but—"

"What the fuck happened?" Jason cries out.

It's been a long day, and he is downright finished with the niceties.

"I understand you're upset; please remain calm, and I'll explain."

Jason scoffs, but throws up his hands and gestures for Bill to continue.

"You see, Jason, things haven't been going well for Jim. He's been having problems with his wife, and it was affecting him here." Bill stops, and Jason can sense he is waiting for him to give some response of understanding, but he isn't giving an inch. So, Bill asks, "Jason, can you understand his situation?"

"You told me he was 'under the weather.' Is it usually common practice for you to lie to your employees on their first day?"

"I am sorry about that. I should've been more honest with you; I was just trying to respect his privacy. But now knowing what he was going through, do you understand his situation?" Bill asks again.

"Oh, I understand alright . . . I understand he's a fucking coward."

"Jason—"

"He fucking quit, Bill! These girls were depending on him, and he fucking quit! What would you call someone who does something like that? Huh? Because I would call them a fucking coward!"

As Jason finishes yelling, he realizes he's now standing and leaning over the table. His arm is raised, and he's aggressively pointing his finger towards Bill in an accusing manner. Jason remains frozen, his hand still shaking, as he looks around frantically. The last ten seconds of his rant are a complete blackout.

"Jason, I need you to take a minute to compose yourself while I lay out our current situation, okay?"

Bill seems unmoved by the outburst, leading Jason to wonder how many times people have screamed at him like that to make him so comfortable with the aggression.

"Okay," Jason responds flatly.

"We are three games into the season, with twelve remaining. Nine of these games are conference games, and they will directly impact whether we add another banner into *The Tunnel of Champions.*" Bill meets Jason's eyeline, making sure he's listening.

"Go on," Jason retorts.

Bill soldiers on. "With Jim leaving, we now—"

"Quitting," Jason interjects.

"Excuse me?"

"You just used the word *leaving*, but Jim didn't *leave*. He *quit.*"

"Eh, semantics . . . am I right?"

There is a hint of levity in Bill's response, and Jason can tell he's trying to diffuse the tension, but he is not amused.

"No, not semantics, Bill. When Jim accepted the position of head coach, he agreed to watch over these girls. To help them grow. To strengthen their confidence and make them feel like they can accomplish anything. Instead, he decided to abandon them."

"Okay, you're right," Bill replies. "With Jim *quitting*, we now need to fill his position, and we need to do it fast. With conference games fast approaching, any small hiccup sends this program back to square one."

"So, who do you recommend?"

"Well, Jason, I'm recommending *you*."

"Me? You want me to lead the team?"

On paper, the idea isn't that crazy—he's already the assistant coach, so it shouldn't be that big of a jump—but to Jason, it *is* that crazy. Weeks ago, he was a high school boys lacrosse coach, and now a man he just met is suggesting he take over a collegiate women's lacrosse program.

This is fucking mental, he thinks.

"This is fucking mental," he says aloud, leading Bill to let out a laugh, and Jason does the same. It's a slightly manic laugh, but a laugh nonetheless.

"Listen, I know this is a lot to take in, but, Jason, I believe in you, and I think you can do this."

"Sir . . . you just met me."

"That may be true, and it certainly won't be easy, but this team needs a leader. Will you accept that responsibility?"

"You know the team won't like this, right?"

"Change is hard, especially at their age, but give them time, and I'm sure they'll see what I see."

This gives Jason a sense of calm as he suddenly realizes why he feels so comfortable around Bill—he reminds him of Chuck. The way he stays level-headed in the face of Jason spiraling, and the way he can use just a few words, but still have a profound impact.

"Alright, I'm in. What's next?"

"Well, next we need to tell the team."

"Would you mind if I did it by myself? If I'm going to win this team over, they need to see me as a leader who can handle things on his own."

"I think that's a fine idea," Bill says. "Jim used to communicate with the team through a sports communication app called *Sports-Chat*. I'll send you the link so you can call the meeting. If I were you, I'd give the team the night off and schedule it for tomorrow morning to tell them the news."

"Sounds like a great plan. I know I could use a night to decompress," Jason replies with a smirk. And with that, he shakes Bill's hand and exits the room.

***

Jenny sits in the locker room, quietly thinking to herself, while the rest of the team stands and argues around her about why they've been called in on their day off. Her mind is racing as well, but she always prided herself on being cool, calm, and collected during times of uncertainty. In those times, she spoke only when the words she had to say would add value to the situation. A trait that she can't help but realize her teammates are severely lacking in this moment as she listens to them squabble around her. Most of the voices just blend together in a loud amalgam of white noise, but some can be heard louder than others.

"What the hell is going on?" Maddy demands.

"Yeah, what the hell is going on?" Nicole echoes.

Twins . . . Am I right? Jenny thinks.

Nicole continues, "And why the hell is the new guy calling a meeting on our day off?"

Sam is quick to jump in: "I'll tell you why; he's a little beta-coach who got power-hungry yesterday. I bet he just wants to apologize to us. He doesn't have the stomach, or the balls, to be a leader."

At this point, Jenny decides she's heard enough. "Sam! He's our coach. Can you at least try to show some respect?"

"LOL—not my coach," Sam replies.

"Sam, those comments are getting a bit old, don't you think?"

"What can I say, I keep it real. Unlike you . . . you whiny little kiss-ass."

The arguing in the room sharply fades into murmurs as Jenny rises to her feet and steps toward Sam.

"Oh shit . . ."

"They're gonna fight . . ."

"This is bad . . ."

Jenny can hear the whispers as she chooses her next words carefully: "Sam, I'm going to give you a chance to take that back, since clearly you weren't raised with any manners."

Sam takes a step toward Jenny. "Oh yeah? What are you going to do about it . . . kiss-ass?"

The quiet murmurs cease as the room goes dead silent. Sam's face is only inches away from Jenny's now as they give each other a death stare, each one waiting to see who will make the first move. The tension rises with every second that passes, as neither player chooses to back down. Just when Jenny can sense the situation is about to collapse into chaos, the locker room door flies open with a bang. The sudden noise startles the players, and all eyes shift from Jenny and Sam to the man standing in the doorway: Jason Nash. Jenny can tell he's concerned as he takes in the situation in front of him. He shakes his head, letting out a deep, frustrated sigh. "Ladies, have a seat."

***

As Jason approaches the locker room, he is still trying to decide exactly how he wants to break the news. He spent the entire night working out the best way to do it. *Should I just be blunt and state the facts, then leave? Should I tell them in smaller groups? Should I go around the room and have everyone share their thoughts on the news?*

Jason is now directly outside the locker room. As he stands there, it occurs to him that no matter how strategic he is in telling the team, it will still probably be a complete disaster. With that hopeless thought, he places his hand on the door and opens it.

He receives no comfort from the scene he walks into as the doors swing open. Jenny and Sam are staring daggers at each other in the center of the room, and he can feel the tension in the air. *Well, I guess this meeting turning into a complete disaster has come sooner than I expected,* he thinks, as he shakes his head and lets out a deep, frustrated sigh before speaking. "Ladies, have a seat."

As everyone sits down, the room remains quiet until Jason hears a voice chime out from the corner of the room. "C-coach . . .?"

It's a voice Jason hasn't heard yet, and his eyes shift over to see who spoke. In the corner sits a girl with shimmering blonde hair and bright blue eyes. She has a thin build, and Jason can see she's nervously picking at the tape that is wrapped around the end of her goalie stick.

Okay, so there's my goalie, he thinks as he realizes he still hasn't officially met most of the team that surrounds him.

"Hi, my name is Chloe. Why . . . are we . . . um . . . Why are we here?"

Jason can sense her uncertainty, and possibly a twinge of worry in her reply. "Very nice to meet you, Chloe." She greets his acknowledgement with a shy smile. "I know you all must be a bit confused about why I called you all in on your day off, so I'll get right to it. Coach Dickerson"—Jason stops to look around the room, surveying the faces of everyone around him—"he quit. I can't give you the specifics, but the headline is that he will no longer be your head coach."

The players look around in bewilderment as they mull over what they've just heard.

"Wait, what?"

"He quit?"

"Is this for real?"

Jason goes to speak again, in an effort to keep the conversation productive and civil, but he is beaten to the punch.

"This is bullshit!" Sam shouts above the rest.

Well, so much for productive and civil.

"Listen, I get it. This is a lot to take in, and the situation is not ideal. But this *is* the situation, and we will handle it together."

"Wait, what do you mean *we* will handle it together? What are *you* going to do to fix this?"

"Well, Sam"—Jason pauses, knowing his next words will most definitely be greeted with opposition—"effective immediately, I will be your new head coach."

A few short gasps reverberate around the room as a shocked look crosses Sam's face. "No. Just no," she replies flatly.

Andddd there's the opposition.

Jason's patience is running thin as he decides what to say next. So far, Sam has found every way to push his buttons, and he is doing his best not to lose his cool, but it is getting harder and harder to do so.

"Sam, this is happening. So, if anyone else in this room has something to say that isn't centered around anger, I would love to hear it."

Jason gets a strange feeling of déjà vu as all twenty-two pairs of eyes stare back at him, just as they had the day before when they first met.

"What does this mean moving forward?" Jenny says, interrupting his thoughts.

Finally, a productive statement.

"Well, it won't actually change that muc—"

"This isn't fair," Maddy interjects.

Nicole, now feeling the need to express her views, says, "Yeah, why don't we get a say in all this? She's right; this isn't fair."

This final comment pushes Jason over the edge.

"Fair? Listen, I can't be the first to tell you all that life isn't fair. You're not always going to like the hand you're dealt. In fact, there will be times when it feels like life is a constant and neverending beatdown of failure and loss. Day in and day out, life can, and will, kick the shit out of you for no reason at all, and the moment you catch a small break and feel like you're finally coming up for air . . . that's when life will double down and run you over like a fucking freight train."

Jason stops and takes a minute to examine the pale faces that sit before him. He can tell some of them want to say something, but no words are coming out, so he moves on and continues sharing what he feels they need to hear. "During these moments, when life has chosen you as its punching bag, how you choose to respond will truly define you. We have five days until our next game, so you need to ask yourself this . . . Do you want to quit, or do you want to try? Do you want to wallow in the things you can't control, or do you want to push through and fight? Because if this is all too much for you, let me know and we can either talk it out or you can say goodbye to this team and simply walk away. But, ladies, make no mistake, this is one of those times when you need to decide what is most important to you. This is where you either persevere through adversity, or you give up and relent."

Jason stops. Looking out upon his team, he feels a sense of pride at the recognition that this may be the first time he has every player's true and undivided attention.

This pride disappears quickly as Sam speaks up. "What could you possibly know about adversity and pain?"

The words hit Jason's ears like a ton of bricks, penetrating his brain and making his body tense uncontrollably. As his fingers press hard into the tattoo on his wrist and his eyes glaze over with a fiery stillness, he takes a long, slow breath through his nose before he responds. "Tomorrow. 8 a.m. Come ready to play, or don't come at all."

No one says anything back; even Sam seems at a loss for words. Jason knows there's nothing more to say, so he exits the room calmly, then stops briefly outside the door as it closes behind him. His inner thoughts are running wild.

Did that go well? Did I come on too strong? What will tomorrow bring?

As he pushes those voices out, forcing them to go quiet, only one thought remains: *Fuck it, can't turn back now.*

CHAPTER 7

Beep, beep, beep, beep. Jason snaps awake at the sound of his alarm going off and slams the snooze button. It's 6 a.m., and as he slowly lifts himself to a sitting position and lets out a massive yawn, he ponders how much sleep he actually got last night. *Three, maybe four hours tops.* His eyes are still adjusting to the light as the sun peeks in through the shades. There's a fan pointed towards the window, causing one single shade to swing back and forth like a metronome. The hum of the fan and the swaying motion of the shade create a hypnotizing effect that he can't seem to take his eyes off of. As it moves back and forth and he fixates on the sun shining in, his mind wanders to a distant memory, and his body collapses back to sleep.

It's a warm, sunny day as Jason exits the front seat of his parents' car, with his sister not far behind. At ten years old, they are both entering fifth grade, and, in order to get them interested in an activity that would keep them outside and active, their mom has taken them to a local sporting goods store. As they approach the front of the building, the large automatic doors slide open. Both Jason and his sister instinctively hold up their hands toward the doors, pretending they're using the Force from *Star Wars*; it's their favorite movie, and they love watching it so much that their parents often joke they should've named them Luke and Leia. After the doors open, Jason locks eyes with his sister, and they both laugh hysterically as they bolt inside the store.

"No running, kids!" their mom yells at them.

"Okay, Mom! You got it!" he yells back. They slow to a fast-paced walk until they round a corner out of their mom's sight. At this point, they give each other a look, smile, and then take off running again.

Jason's face is beaming, making his cheeks hurt, as they skip through the hat section of the store, aisle by aisle, trying on everything around them.

"How's this one look, Sis?" he says to her as he puts on a bright blue *Manchester City* hat that is way too big for his head. The brim sits so low it covers half his face.

"Hmm . . ." she replies, jokingly pretending to think it over. A large smirk forms across her face when she can't keep up the charade any longer. She throws up her hands with thumbs pointed to the sky. "Two thumbs-up, Jay."

When they were both just learning to speak, Jason's sister was struggling to form words greater than one syllable, so when she went to say his name all that came out was "Jay." At first, their parents were concerned it was a learning disability, but she eventually corrected the problem as time went on. "Jay," however, was a nickname that stuck.

Jason keeps looking over the hats neatly laid out on the shelves before him, his neck craning as he tries to see the ones sitting on the top shelf. He grabs another one in front of him, this one even larger than the one before, and places it atop his head, in an effort to garner an even bigger laugh from his sister.

"Okay, Sis. How abou—" As he turns around to see her reaction, he stops short when he notices she is nowhere to be seen. He removes the hat and looks up and down the aisle before his eyes narrow with understanding. Normally, his sister disappearing would be a scary thought, but he knows her all too well. This is no accident; this is a game. *Hide-and-go-seek on an epic scale,* he thinks. A large store surrounds him, endless places to hide, so many obstacles to overcome . . . "Game on, Sis," he says aloud, his voice heavy with determination and sprinkled with the innocence of childlike wonder. "Game on."

As Jason walks up and down the store's seemingly endless number of hallways, he searches in every possible location he can think of. He checks inside circular racks of hanging shirts, underneath benches where people would sit to try on shoes, and even behind cash registers where employees are ringing up customers. A little time passes, and a small pit forms in his stomach. *Where could she be?*

After about five more minutes of searching, he picks up his pace, and a sense of worry washes over him. He's still fairly certain this is a game, but he doesn't like being apart from his sister. After a few more minutes, his fear starts to peak until he rounds a corner and sees a row of mannequins lined up down the hallway, displaying various trendy sporting outfits. As he observes them, he notices the fourth "mannequin" down the line to be about three feet shorter than the rest, and it is shaking nervously as it attempts to stand as still as possible. Jason lets out a sigh of relief as he slows to a walk and approaches the first mannequin, inspecting it intently.

"Yup, that one's real," he says loudly, for the benefit of his sister to hear. She's still trying her best to stand as still as possible, though it is clearly becoming more challenging with each passing second as she desperately tries to stifle a laugh. Jason moves on to the next mannequin. "Yup, this one's real too."

At this point, his sister is barely holding it together, her whole body shaking from the laughter she is hopelessly trying to hold in while still doing her best to keep up the act. Jason is also attempting to keep a straight face as they both keep on pretending, for no one's amusement other than their own. As he approaches the third mannequin, standing just beside his sister, he stops and takes a more speculative look.

"Aha! I found you!" Jason proclaims, pointing to the lifeless figure standing in front of him. He gives the mannequin's hard plastic leg a slap. "But, Sis, I have to say, you're looking kind of stiff, don't you think?"

At this point, neither of them can keep up the act any longer; they both keel over laughing, their faces sporting massive cheek dimples from the smiles that simply will not fade. Once they catch their breath, Jason looks to his sister. "Alright, what's next?"

They both look around, and at almost exactly the same time, their eyes fall on a giant sign hanging from the ceiling. There are no words on the sign, just pictures of footballs, basketballs, baseballs, and almost every other type of sports-related ball you could think of. They take off running.

When they arrive at the aisle, they both stop short as their heads move from side to side, like slow-moving bobbleheads, taking in their surroundings. Containers full of kickballs sit to their left; soccer balls and basketballs sit neatly displayed on shelves to their right, and pool noodles hang from the top shelf at the end of the aisle. For Jason and his sister, this is heaven.

Jason's sister is the first to make her move. She runs over to the kickballs and has to stand on her tippy-toes to reach inside the container. After struggling for a moment, she manages to pull one out, and she doesn't hesitate to toss it into the air and kick it as hard as she can down the aisle, with no concern for what lies ahead. The ball makes a loud *boing* as it leaves her foot and flies down the hallway. It bounces harmlessly off a shelf before flying uncontrollably in the opposite direction, smashing into one of two large football displays at the end of the aisle and causing at least a dozen of them to fall to the floor below. With each football that hits the ground, a loud *thud* echoes in the store, making Jason and his sister wince. After a few seconds, all the balls have fallen, and Jason's sister turns towards him, moving cautiously, before slowly lifting her index finger to her lips. "Shhhh . . ." she says with a grin, fighting the urge to giggle.

Jason laughs with her as his eyes shift to his right, and he grabs the closest soccer ball he can find. He places it on the ground and attempts to mimic exactly what she just did. He kicks the ball with vigor, but it falls hopelessly short of the second football display, failing to accomplish his goal of creating even more destruction at the end of the aisle.

Jason looks around and tries to find something else that he could use to devise possible carnage within this unsuspecting hallway, but his sister quickly interrupts his attempt. "Hey, Jay!"

Jason looks over to his sister and sees she is standing beneath a large number of three-foot metal poles hanging above her. The sign above each pole reads "Lacrosse Sticks." Jason doesn't have the slightest idea what *lacrosse* is, but as he stares at the word and aimlessly contemplates its meaning, his sister tosses him a stick.

Jason admires it, entranced by its bright blue color, its lightweight feel, and even the three large letters printed on the side, "STX," which he assumes must be some weird brand name he's never heard of. Seconds later, the spell of the stick is broken when his sister says, "If you're not with me, then you're my enemy . . ."

Jason is somewhat confused until he looks up and sees his sister holding up a bright red stick in the unmistakable manner of a Sith Lord. Quickly picking up on the *Star Wars* movie quote, Jason doesn't miss a beat. He raises his bright blue stick in the same imposing manner and replies, "Only a Sith deals in absolutes . . . I will do what I must."

"You will try!" she responds, and they both run at each other, swinging the sticks back and forth, making lightsaber noises with their mouths every time the sticks collide.

"Kksssshh! Kksssshh!" they both yell as the sticks clang together.

After a few more swings of the pretend "sabers," they slam them together one more time and hold them in place. Their faces are inches apart, and they're both pretending to struggle as they hold them there, feigning the tension of the situation.

"You were the chosen one!" Jason screams, and they both collapse to the ground, cackling loudly, their faces beet red from laughter.

Seconds later, their mom walks around the corner and bears witness to the chaotic scene around them: the footballs still lying carelessly on the ground, the kickball and soccer ball sitting innocently next to them, and her two children roaring with laughter in the center of it all. "Kids! What did you do?"

Both Jason and his sister stop and look at their mother. She just stares at them, with her eyes wide and mouth agape, revealing her shock and bewilderment. They then glance back at each other and start laughing even harder than they were before. Without a care in the world, Jason just lies there on the dirty tile floor next to his sister, his mind free and full of joy.

Beep, beep, beep, beep! Jason jolts awake and slams his alarm clock again to stop the incessant ringing. His breathing is rapid, and sweat is now dripping from his brow. The clock reads 6:09 a.m., and Jason sits up in bed again, this time swinging his legs out from under the covers to make sure he doesn't drift back off to dreamland. *Nine minutes of bliss. I guess that's all I get today,* he thinks, letting out a long, arduous groan and thrusting himself out of bed.

CHAPTER 8

As the sun rises over the eastern bleachers and a brilliant red-orange hue emanates from the sky, it beams down to the field and lights up the lime-green turf in an exceptionally complementary way. Jason stands in the center of the field, taking in the blissful sight before him, before glancing down at his watch to check the time: 7:48 a.m. With every minute that passes, his anxiety spikes just a little as he anticipates the double doors slamming open, signifying the team is about to take the field. He's not nervous, per se, but in the last two days, he has already grown to expect some pushback from the team—or at least from a small segment of the team—but even for a small group, they certainly know how to cause a great deal of friction.

Two days . . . I've only been here for two freaking days.

As he shakes his head in amazement and recollects just how much has changed in the last forty-eight hours, he smirks at the thought. Jason can hear Chuck's voice clearly in his head:

"Sometimes, the only way to get through painful times is to laugh at your pain."

"Ain't that the truth," Jason says aloud.

Slam!

The doors swing open, and Jason watches as the team strolls out two by two in his direction. He counts twenty-two approaching, and a small sense of relief surges through his body. It's not that he expected anyone to not show up, but it's nice to know his slightly brash words yesterday didn't deter any of them from coming. As they approach, they aren't as chatty as usual, but it's 8 a.m. on a Monday morning, so Jason assumes fairly confidently that this is the reason for their lack of energy as they walk toward him. Once they all gather around him, he addresses the team: "Good morning!"

They acknowledge his greeting with what can only be described as bitter, discontented groans.

Yup, not morning people.

"In a few short days, we will be taking on Brighton Banks University. I looked over your history of playing against them, and I watched some film from their game this past Wednesday." He takes a beat to observe their reaction, hoping to be greeted with looks of gratification at the effort he is putting in, but they're giving him nothing.

Oh, well, chalk that up to the early morning as well.

He presses on. "It seems to me that you've never had any trouble beating them in the past, and I don't foresee any reason this game should be any different after reviewing their recent film. However—"

"Here we fucking go," Sam mutters under her breath, but still very much vocal enough for the people around her to hear.

Jason notices the twins look at her with a smirk.

"Excuse me, Sam? You got something you want to say?"

"No, I have nothing to say to you," she replies, which does surprise Jason—her tone is still brazen, but it seems a lot less condescending than her previous statements over the last two days.

Hmm . . . maybe this is also due to the early morning. I should do this more often.

"Okay, then, as I was saying, today will be a typical day of practice, nothing crazy. But, as always, we'll begin with a lap of the field to warm up those legs."

The team takes off, and Jason signals for Jenny to stay with him again. He is still woefully lacking in knowledge of the team he is now in charge of, and he wants some more insight into the players he now has to lead.

"What's up, Coach?" Jenny gets straight to business.

Jason isn't sure what he likes more, the fact that she gets right to the point, or the fact that she refers to him as *coach*, which to

Sam would apparently be the equivalent of saying "Beetlejuice" three times.

"I was hoping you could give me a very brief 'bio,' if you will, on the remaining members of the team that we didn't get to discuss on Saturday."

"For sure," she replies, then lifts her head and scans the line of players circling the field. "The girl in the front there with the goalie stick—that's Chloe."

"Oh, right, she spoke up yesterday in the locker room. She seemed a little nervous, but I assumed that was just because of the impromptu meeting."

"Yes, truthfully, though, I think it's more than that. She's a first-year, and ever since our senior goalie quit the team over winter break, she was kind of *thrown into the fire*, if you will. Which is great for experience, but as you know, we're 0–3 through our first three games, and she's been taking it fairly personally."

"It can't all be the goalie's fault," Jason replies.

"True, and it's not all her fault. But when things start to go south, Sam isn't someone who jumps at the opportunity to take responsibility, and she can get a bit nasty toward Chloe when she lets a goal in."

"Doesn't Chloe understand that if another team takes a shot on goal, that means our defense didn't do their job well enough?" Jason points out.

"She does, but when a senior captain yells at you as a first-year, it can be challenging to defend yourself." Jason can hear the distress in her voice—she feels for Chloe.

"Okay, got it." Jason decides to move the conversation along after seeing the team is nearly finished with their lap. "How about the midfielders?"

"Well, to be honest, there are only six really solid midfielders. The rest are okay and could be subbed on in a pinch, but personally, I wouldn't recommend it," Jenny states flatly. "Not that I'm telling you how to coach, Coach."

"It's okay, Jenny. I wouldn't have asked for your opinion if I didn't want an honest one. Who are the six strongest middies?"

"They like to run together towards the end of the line, see?" Jenny points to the tail end of the pack. "The first three are Rachel, Taya, and Luna. Rachel and Taya both came from the same high school, so they knew each other coming in, and they work well together. That being said, Rachel is definitely a tad more reserved than Taya; she also doesn't ever like to swear."

"No shit?" Jason muses, leading to a small grin from Jenny. "And Luna?"

"Luna actually meshed pretty seamlessly with them, but she is more of the strong, silent type. She doesn't speak a lot; instead, she lets her game do the talking, and her game is good, Coach, just wait and see."

"And the other three?"

"Daisy, Dahlia, and Dakotah. And no, I'm not making that up," Jenny replies with a chuckle.

"For real?"

"Yup, for real, Coach. Three strong players, kind of cliquey, but not in a negative way. They just really enjoy being around each other, both on and off the field."

"Well, alright, then. Daisy, Dahlia, Dakotah . . . I do love some good alliteration," Jason replies, just as the team is finishing up and filters in around him. He still doesn't have intel on everyone, but he's making progress. *Brick by brick.*

"Here's how today is going to go," Jason announces. "We will practice as a team. Everybody does every drill, no exceptions. We'll start with one-on-ones, and I want you all getting offensive reps."

"Fucking why?" an all too familiar voice calls out.

"Well, Sam, you never know what could occur in a game. You may find yourself on the offensive side of the field with very little time left on the clock, and if that happens, I need to know you'll have what it takes to deliver."

"Why would I ever be on the offensive side of the field?"

I guess the early morning isn't slowing her down anymore.

"You know, Sam, for someone who plays defense, you sure like to go on the offensive in these conversations."

"Ooooh shit . . ."

"No way . . ."

"This man's got gall . . ."

The whispers reverberate throughout the circle of players. As a coach, he isn't super proud of what he just said, but as a fed-up human being, he is.

The whispers continue to hum until Sam shoots a sharp look in their direction, with fierce unblinking eyes, and they immediately cease. *She may be rude, but she commands the group with just a look . . . Yup, she's a captain,* Jason thinks. With that lone thought of admiration, the practice commences.

For the full two hours that follow, it still remains a similar struggle for Jason. Yes, he is officially their head coach, and a few more players have gotten on board, giving him their attention and some semblance of respect. But others—namely Sam, The Shady Sisters, and a few more players who may have also adopted that same "let's be contrarian" attitude—still refuse to take him seriously. While Jason takes note of this constant friction, he can only assume it will all come to a head in some large, melodramatic way that will either make or break his progress. Soon after, this is no longer an assumption.

"Last but not least, we're going to practice shooting. And yes, everyone is going to get an opportunity to take shots on goal, even the defense," Jason announces, looking very pointedly in Sam's direction, trying to get ahead of any resentment she may choose to add.

"With all due respect, sir . . ." Sam says.

Looks like I won't be avoiding that resentment after all . . . Still, at least she used the word 'respect,' Jason thinks.

"Why should we listen to a man who has never picked up a women's lacrosse stick in his life?"

Well, there goes that respect . . .

Jason stops to think, considering just having the team run more sprints, but he decides to take a different approach. "Sam, have you ever played Horse?"

"Duh. Of course I have, why?"

"Well, I was wondering if you'd like to play a quick game against me?"

"Umm, listen, guy, I know you don't know me, but even though I don't play offense, I've still got a mean shot . . . This shit wouldn't even be fair." Jason can hear the confidence in her voice rising as she looks around at the group for approval.

"Okay, then let's make things interesting. We'll go shot for shot. The first person to make a mistake loses and has to run ten, full field sprints, down and back."

An audible reaction ripples throughout the team, so Jason doubles down. "Unless you're too scared?"

Sam's face goes blank, and Jason can tell she's doing her best to hide the frustration that is boiling up inside. "Your funeral . . . Top-right corner."

She picks up a ball lying in front of her and effortlessly pins the top-right corner. Jason tries to hide his admittedly impressed facial expression. "Not bad," he states as he walks over to Dahlia and reaches for her stick. "Do you mind if I borrow this?"

"Uhh, yeah. Sure thing, Coach."

She is now full of curiosity as she hands over the lacrosse stick. Without hesitation, Jason scoops up a ball and pins the same top corner with ease.

"Shit." The word just slips out of Dahlia's mouth, and she immediately brings her hand up and covers her face. "Sorry, Coach, I didn't mean to swear."

"That's okay, Dahlia; it was impressive, no?"

Jason adds a healthy dose of sarcasm to try and mask the narcissism that he knows is all too present.

"Lucky," Sam says flatly before grabbing a ball and ripping it again towards the net. As she releases the shot, she calls out, "Top left."

Again, the ball lands exactly where she'd wanted it to, firmly in the top-left corner. The murmurs among the team grow louder, but Jason shuts them down with an immediate replication of Sam's shot.

"Listen, I know some of you have class soon, so why don't I end this now, okay?" Jason says aloud.

"What, you want to end the game?"

"No, Sam, I'm *going* to end the game." The team looks around at each other as he says, "Crossbar, crossbar, crossbar, crossbar, crossbar."

"What?"

The single word is all Sam can get out before Jason picks up another ball and proceeds to literally play pass with himself off the 1-inch thick crossbar that makes up the top segment of the goal. Twenty-two faces stare blankly back at him—an occurrence that is now becoming a habit—and he hands Dahlia back her stick as he walks toward Sam.

"I know I don't know you, Sam . . . but you don't know me either." His voice is low yet imposing, and he waits a beat before adding, "Now why don't you break us down, Captain . . . And don't forget, you owe me some sprints."

She looks back at him with unblinking eyes, clearly weighing a response, before begrudgingly lifting her stick to the sky. "Sticks up!" she demands, and the team follows her command.

While Jason turns away to leave them to it, he catches a few players staring at him with their eyebrows raised in curiosity. He knows they're trying to figure him out, and that brings a smile to his face. Behind him, the team chants, "Jays on three—one, two, three, Jays!"

Afterwards, he sits down on the sideline bench and does his best to relax as he watches Sam run her sprints. Back and forth . . .

Back and forth . . . Back and forth . . . There's an almost poetic parallel between her motion and that of his window shade this morning, going back and forth like a metronome, with the sunny morning sky as a backdrop.

Chapter 9

Cling-cling!

The small brass bell above the heavy wooden door chimes as Jason heaves it open. When he steps inside the establishment, the high-end air conditioning unit above the door activates, giving a satisfying cooling effect on Jason's now sunburnt skin.

After practice earlier in the day, he stayed at the field an extra thirty minutes to watch Sam finish her sprints, and then he headed into his office to get some more work done. He wanted to create a practice plan for the rest of the week that would get everyone on the team more involved—it had occurred to him that, although he was making decent progress with some of the players, he was still struggling to coach such a large group of people effectively, and with their next game only days away, he was desperate to come up with a solution. In addition to the practice plan, he also wanted to watch more film of Brighton Banks University.

After about five hours of work, his brain felt like mush, and he simply couldn't look at a computer screen any longer, so he decided to call it quits for the day. On his way out, he passed another coach in the hallway. Jason wasn't sure who they were, or even what sport they coached, but that didn't stop them from opening up a dialogue: "How are you doing tonight, Coach?" they said.

To which Jason jokingly replied, "I need a drink."

He chuckled under his breath as the words came out of his mouth, but the other coach didn't miss a beat. "You should try The Iron Penn; it's a local bar about three blocks off campus. They've got great beer and nice whiskey!"

"Say no more," Jason replied, always a sucker for a good, aged whiskey.

As he walks into the bar only an hour after that conversation, he notices rather quickly that it is not what he expected. Jason had pictured a typical towny bar with loud music, sticky floors, and maybe a few overzealous drunks. But this bar is not like that at all. The floor is made of beautifully stained hardwood; the circular light fixtures that hang from the ceiling are big and bright, and the bar appears clean and is composed of a single slab of marble that must weigh more than a ton.

Even the servers are not what he expected. Each one is wearing a sleek gray uniform that bears the name *The Iron Penn* in bright white letters over the left breast pocket. These servers roam around the place, moving with a purpose, every step they take seeming calculated and thought out. The lone bartender is tall, with long dark hair pulled back into a tight bun, and she's wearing a stylish pin-striped three-piece suit to complete the look.

After taking it all in, Jason chooses a plush maroon stool at the corner of the bar to sit at, then pulls his phone from his pocket. The practice plan is still very much on his mind, and he figures if anyone can crack the code on how to train a large group of players properly in a short period of time, it's Chuck.

Jason dials the number, puts the phone to his ear, and waits. *Ring, ring . . . Ring, ring . . . Ring, ring . . . "Hey, it's Chuck; leave a message at the beep."* Jason hangs up. He doesn't feel like leaving a message, and he knows Chuck will call back. Once he places the phone back in his pocket, it isn't long before the bartender approaches.

"Good evening, sir, what'll you have?"

She's objectively gorgeous, and her eyes are a stunning blue in contrast to her jet-black hair.

"Can I get an old-fashioned?"

"Any particular whiskey you're looking for?"

"Dealer's choice. Unless you happen to have a Glenfiddich 15 Year back there?"

The bartender lets out a small grin and reaches under the bar to reveal a tall, dark purple cylinder. The words *Glenfiddich 15* are branded on the front, and it sports the signature golden stag logo.

"A man who knows what he likes. I admire that," she replies. "You're new around here, aren't you?"

"How'd you know?"

"There aren't many locals walking in here looking for the good stuff." She points to the bottle. "That's why I had this bad boy under the bar."

"What can I say, I like a good whiskey," he replies with a smile, leading her to let out a lighthearted chuckle before grabbing the ingredients and creating the cocktail.

Jason is entranced by the way she moves as she does it. Every motion is fluid and effortless as she first mixes simple syrup and a few dashes of bitters into a large mixing glass towering with ice. Next, she uncorks the bottle of whiskey and empties a healthy pour into the glass—she doesn't use a measuring jigger, but somehow Jason is sure she's nailed the ratio correctly. She then inserts a long silver spoon into the combination of liquids and stirs it in a clockwise direction about a dozen times; each time it circles the rim, he becomes more and more hypnotized by the action. Once the ingredients are sufficiently blended together, she pours the concoction over a single large ice cube that sits perfectly nestled inside a textured crystal glass in front of her. The liquid rises just to the edge of the rim, and to finish, she squeezes one flat sliver of an orange peel over the top of it, and a citrus mist sprays out over the entire glass.

After dropping in the peel, she places the drink on a slate coaster in front of Jason. "Here you are, sir."

"Jason," he responds. "The name's Jason."

"Nice to meet you, Jason. I'm Lucy."

He gives her a nod and smiles, and then he picks up the drink and takes a sip. As the old-fashioned touches his tongue, the flavors all meld together and coat his taste buds. A chill goes down his spine, and his brain leaps back eight years to his twenty-first birthday, when Chuck had bought him his first drink—this drink. Jason pulls the glass away from his lips and swallows before blurting out, "Fuck me, that's good."

After the words fall from his mouth, he looks at Lucy, a bit embarrassed. It probably isn't the classiest look to be dropping f-bombs at a nice establishment like this one. Her reaction, however, is not what he expects, as she breaks out laughing and her face turns bright red.

"Glad you like it, Jason," she replies with a grin. "Let me know if you need anything else, okay?"

"Sure thing," he says, and she leaves to tend to other customers.

While Jason sits there, it hits him that this is the first time since he arrived in Pittsburgh that he's felt even remotely welcomed by the city, and also the first time he hasn't felt worried about what comes next. With that thought in mind, he takes another sip of his drink and surveys his surroundings. The bar's fairly packed; most of the tables are occupied by a variety of different patrons. There's a family of four at a nearby table that appears to be celebrating some sort of achievement, though Jason isn't sure what it is. Next to them is what he believes to be a married couple—as they're both wearing wedding rings—but neither one of them is talking; they're just staring down at their phones, scrolling away.

At the end of the bar is a group of guys that Jason is sure are local college kids. They're ordering beers one after another, and putting them down just as fast. What impresses Jason the most is that while it does seem very busy, it's not a *chaotic* kind of busy. Everything seems to be running smoothly. The waitstaff is taking orders quickly and being extremely courteous to their guests, even when the people they're serving don't offer them the same respect. The workers who are bussing tables seem to be working at an impressive pace as well, clearing the tables with extreme efficiency.

As Jason continues to take in his surroundings, he notices something he hadn't before. While every member of the staff, aside from Lucy, is wearing a gray uniform—they also appear to have small patches sewn into the sleeves of the shirts. The servers have a red patch; the bussers have a yellow patch, and the hostess has a green patch. Every patch contains small words written on it, but Jason can't quite make out what they say. Out of nothing more than humble curiosity, he signals Lucy.

"Yes, Jason, what can I do for you?"

"I was wondering if you know why all the workers here are wearing those patches on their arms, and what they mean?"

"Well, as a matter of fact, I might be the best person to answer that question."

Jason raises an eyebrow. "And why is that?"

"Because, Jason, I actually own this bar, so I manage all of these employees, and I'm the one who gave them the uniforms."

"No shit?" Jason replies, which again gets a small grin out of Lucy.

He gets the sense that she isn't someone who would shy away from using curse words, except while at work, of course.

"No shit, indeed," she says.

Ha, I guess she isn't worried about swearing at work after all.

"So, what's the deal with the patches?"

"Well, each one signifies a different job. Red is for servers, and those patches read *Infantry*. Yellow is for bussers, and those patches read *Transport*. Green is for the hostess, and that patch reads *Vanguard*."

"Are those military terms?"

"Yes, they are; my mom was in the marines for thirty years before she retired this past January."

Jason goes to speak, but Lucy cuts him off, as if she already knows what he wants to ask next.

"I gave those specific military terms to each group of my staff so they'd feel like they were part of a team. It's no secret that restaurant work isn't the most glamorous profession, so feeling like you're part of an elite squad—it makes the job more enjoyable. Plus, it makes them feel pretty badass too."

Jason sits in awe. He never imagined so much thought could go into what he considered to be a fairly menial job. At first, all he can say is, "That's incredible." But then he adds, "Let me ask you this though . . . How did you get them all to work so efficiently? I mean, this might truly be the smoothest-running bar I've ever been to."

"I'm flattered," she replies, then picks up an empty glass next to him. "Honestly, it's all about how you train them."

"What do you mean?"

"Well, in total, I have twelve employees that I manage. There are three hostesses, three bussers, and six servers. I discovered early on that it's way easier to train them in smaller groups than it is to try and train them all at once. They're more focused on what you're trying to teach them, and also, let's face it, a busser isn't too concerned with what a hostess has to do, and vice versa."

"Train them in small groups . . ." Jason says to himself. "Huh, that's brilliant, thank you."

"You're welcome, although I'm not quite sure what you're thanking me for."

"For . . ." He pauses, eyeing his empty glass. "For the best old-fashioned I've had in a long time."

Her face becomes slightly flushed as she opens her mouth to respond, but she's interrupted by a *roar* of laughter from a room just around the corner from the bar.

"What's in there?" Jason asks.

"That's our luxury lounge that people can reserve for private parties, corporate events, and things like that. Actually, before you go, here's my card." She hands him a matte black business card with the words *The Iron Penn,* and the bar's phone number, printed neatly in the center. "If you ever want to host your own event, feel free to give me a call."

Jason focuses on the card between his fingers, fairly certain there's no possible reason he'll ever need to rent a private room, but he sticks it in his wallet anyway, to be polite.

"Thank you, I'll be sure to do that!" he replies, then tosses thirty dollars in cash on the table to pay for the drink. "I've gotta run; keep the change."

"Great taste *and* you're a good tipper? You'd better find your way back here again, Jason."

Her voice has a hint of flirtatiousness, but Jason thinks nothing of it. *She's probably just being nice.*

"Oh, don't you worry, Lucy, I'll be back. And thanks again; you've helped me a lot tonight . . . more than you know."

Her face tilts, but she doesn't respond; she just smiles as Jason turns and walks toward the door. While he swings it open—and the air conditioning unit kicks on and blasts him from above—his phone vibrates from inside his pocket. After retrieving his phone, he checks the caller ID and sees that it's Chuck calling.

Right on cue, he thinks, then answers the call. "Hey, Chuck, thanks for calling back."

"Jason, buddy, sorry I missed your call. I was in a meeting, and I'm just getting out now."

"That's okay, I was just calling for some advice about a problem I was having at practice."

"Oh yeah? What's the problem? I'll see if I can help."

"Well, actually, Chuck . . . I think I figured it out."

CHAPTER 10

Jason opens his car door and steps out into the cool morning that awaits. It's 7:30 a.m. on a Friday, and the air is still. He closes the car door and walks across the empty parking lot, thinking back to the past three days of practice.

Breaking up the team into smaller groups had been a stroke of genius, as it gave him the chance to really dive in and properly coach each player and their respective positions.

Thanks for that, Lucy.

Giving each position a nickname had also been a fun tool to liven up practice. The defense was *The Brick Wall*; he called the midfielders *The Soldiers,* and he called his attackers *The Arsenal.* "Thanks for that, too," he says aloud, with Lucy in mind.

The soft sound of mourning doves hits his ears as he strolls toward the field and enjoys the tranquility of the world around him. The atmosphere is hushed and peaceful, and his mind feels calm and free as his eyes wander and land on the row of weeping willows that border the parking lot. Their bright green branches droop down in a sad but graceful way, and the silver-tipped leaves help to add beauty to the tree's already elegant form.

Dink!

The sudden noise startles Jason and jolts his brain back to reality. *What was that?*

As he stops walking to listen. He waits for a moment but hears nothing. Assuming he must've imagined the noise, he starts walking again.

Dink!

There it is again! What the hell is that?

He keeps moving toward the field, and shortly after, he hears it again.

Dink!

Is it coming from the field?

Dink!

Yes, it's definitely coming from the field.

Jason picks up his pace toward the gate that leads to the turf. With every step he takes, the noise persists, and grows louder. Finally, he reaches the gate and swings it open; the rusty hinges let out a light *screech* as he does. Jason looks out to the far end of the field and sees one lone person standing in front of the lacrosse net, with a stick in her hand and a bucket of balls by her side.

Who the hell could that be? No one gets here this early.

Once he gets within about twenty yards of the person, he recognizes her. "Rachel?"

"What the—?" she screams as she turns around, clearly frightened.

"Shit, sorry! I shouldn't have snuck up like that . . . But what are you doing here so early? We have another thirty minutes until practice, and from the looks of it, you've been here a while."

"I got here at 6 a.m."

"What? Why?" is all Jason can say.

"I'm trying to work on my shot. I see the twins pinning corners during practice and in games, and . . . I don't know . . . it makes me feel like I'm not good enough. They just make it look so easy."

"First of all, you don't think you're *good enough*? That is utter nonsense. Rachel, you're a starting midfielder on a Division 1 lacrosse team. You are absolutely *good enough*."

"Okay, fine. But I could be better. And this on-the-run shot I've been working on . . . I just can't seem to get it right."

"Let me see what you've got," Jason replies, pointing to the net.

Rachel reluctantly scoops up another ball that is lying at her feet and moves into position. She takes off running parallel with the net, and when she gets close enough, she fires off a shot on the run.

Dink!

The ball hits the post and ricochets away from the goal.

"Ugh! See!" she yells out, with her hand pointed accusatorially at the net. "I just can't get it right."

Her head drops in anguish.

"So you didn't get it right, is that any reason to give up and stop trying?" Jason responds as she walks back towards him.

"Honestly, it might be. I've been at this for weeks, but I can't seem to master it. Maybe I *should* just give up." The look of distress grows on her face as she waits for Jason's reply.

"Rachel, is this something you truly want to accomplish? Would perfecting this shot bring you satisfaction?"

"Yes. But—"

"No. No *buts*," Jason interrupts. "If this is something that will make you happy, then you can't give up. You owe it to yourself to keep trying."

"But I just keep failing."

"Yes, and you will keep failing, over and over again, until finally . . . you stop failing, and you get it right. That's how life works, Rachel."

"But, Coach, it isn't that easy. Failure sucks . . . I don't know how much more I can handle."

"Rachel, let me ask you something. If you knew you were one hundred failed attempts away from perfecting this shot, how fast would you fail those one hundred times?"

"I mean . . . obviously, I'd do it as fast as possible," she replies. "But, Coach, I don't know how many more failed attempts it's going to take to get this right."

"Exactly. You don't know how close you are, so why stop now?"

Rachel just stands there, processing his words in silent reflection. "I-I guess you're right, Coach. Sorry, I can get in my own head sometimes."

"Happens to the best of us. Just keep at it."

Slam!

The doors to the field open up and the team files out, heading in their direction.

"Well, here we go. Would you mind cleaning up these balls while I get everything started?"

"Sure thing, Coach," Rachel replies, "and thank you."

Jason gives a nod as the rest of the team arrives. He clears his throat before addressing them. "Alright, team, first off, I'd say this has been a productive week, and since we have a game tomorrow, we'll be taking it fairly easy today." A wave of subtle but vocal sighs of relief can be heard. "I'll be setting up stations that you will all rotate through as the practice progresses, and I will circulate from station to station, giving advice as I see fit."

"What advice could you possibly have to give us?"

Jason hadn't really expected Sam to chime in with her negative comments yet, and it catches him off guard. He's right in the middle of taking a sip of water when Jenny speaks up. "Judging from your game of Horse earlier this week, I'd say he could probably teach you how to shoot."

Jason does a spit take as he tries to stifle his laughter—always appreciating a good, well-timed joke.

As a team, they let out a loud and mocking, "*Oooooh,*" before Sam shoots a menacing look at everyone, and the sound ceases.

"Alright, alright, that's enough," Jason says. "We're all here to get ready for the game tomorrow, so let's get to it. My defensive *Brick Wall,* you will all be down at the far end of the field. *The Soldiers* will be here at midfield, and *The Arsenal,* you'll be at the other end."

The team members separate, and Jason approaches Jenny, quietly lifting his hand for a fist bump. "That was nice," he says with a smirk.

She bumps his fist and then turns away, doing her best to hide the smile now present on her face.

The stations Jason created for each group focus on three things: footwork, body positioning, and shooting. As he cycles from group to group, he realizes rather quickly that he's been giving fairly generic advice. "Keep your elbows up." "Make sure to shuffle and keep your hips square." "Always keep your head on a swivel." While this does give him the sense that the team is working efficiently, it also makes him feel somewhat underutilized. Jason wants to make an impact on these players, and simply giving them small pointers on their fundamental game isn't exactly what he would call *game-changing advice.*

Brick by brick, he reminds himself. *Change doesn't happen overnight, and small wins add up.*

While contemplating his coaching progress, he notices Chloe standing alone by the bench area, so he curiously approaches. "Hey, Chloe, what's up?" She turns to him, revealing her red and watery eyes. "Oh, my God. Chloe, what's wrong?"

"N-n-nothing. I-I'm okay," she chokes out, clearly trying to hide the fact that she's upset about something.

"Chloe, have a seat." Jason gestures toward the bench with his hand, and they both sit down. "You know you can trust me, right?"

"Y-yes . . . I know. It's just . . ." She trails off and then wipes away a tear that has rolled down her cheek. "I don't want you to think any less of me."

"Excuse me? Chloe, if I ever thought less of a player because they expressed themselves honestly with me, I'd be a pretty shitty coach, don't you think?" he replies, trying to sound lighthearted in an effort to break down the walls she's put up.

"I-I'm just nervous . . . I haven't played very well in the last few games, and I don't want to keep letting the team down. And I also don't want to let you down, Coach. I'm just afraid I'll make a mistake, that's all."

Jason places a hand on her shoulder and meets her gaze. "Chloe, you've been put in an extremely tough situation. You've been asked to step up as a first-year and perform at the highest level. And I can promise you, it's impossible for you to let anyone down, because you've already done so much for this team." At this point, the tears have stopped, and she is listening intently, so Jason continues, "And as for you being 'afraid to fail,' Chloe, do you know how many high school lacrosse players make the jump to college lacrosse?"

"No."

"Roughly twelve percent. That means about eighty-eight percent of all lacrosse players never get the chance to be sitting where you're sitting right now. So, Chloe, you shouldn't be afraid to fail. You should be afraid of never getting the chance to try."

He finishes speaking, and for a minute, she just stares back at him, as if processing what he said. Then, out of nowhere, she gives him a quick hug. "Thank you. You're a good coach."

Out of the corner of his eye, he catches a glimpse of Sam running by. "At least one of you thinks I am," he states, for both of their amusement. "I know Sam's been hard on you, but don't let her get you down. Some people just struggle to express themselves productively when things get hard."

She nods, then pulls away and heads back onto the field with a new look of determination in her eyes. Jason remains seated, alone on the bench. A smile of fulfillment appears, and his face begins to quiver ever so slightly as one lone tear rolls down his face.

When Jason gets up to return to the field himself, he can see Luna standing about ten feet away, looking in his direction.

Did she hear that?

She meets his gaze, then turns away. He shrugs and walks back toward the center of the field.

Eh, who knows . . . Back to it, I guess.

CHAPTER 11

The sky is beginning to dim as Jason looks over his notes from the past week. Tomorrow is the first time he'll stand on the sideline as a collegiate lacrosse coach, and he can already feel the anxiety kicking in. As he sits alone in his apartment staring down at the sheets of paper before him, the words on the page start to vibrate and his vision blurs. He gives his head a rapid shake and blinks his eyes a few times, hoping to return his mind to the task at hand, but his head feels faint, and now his vision is going white. He quickly drops the papers on his desk and closes his eyes, taking long, deep breaths.

The fear of tomorrow has found its way into his mind. As the muscles in his face become tense, his chest tightens, and he can feel his fingernails digging into his palms while he clenches his fists. "Breathe in, breathe out, breathe in, breathe out," he says repeatedly.

Jason performs this long-winded breathing technique until his mind slowly settles down. Gradually, his body returns to a calmer state, and after a minute or two, he opens his eyes.

"Fuck me . . ." he says to himself, then gently goes to pick up the papers he dropped.

As he places them back in a neat stack on his desk, his phone rings; he checks the caller ID and sees that it's Chuck calling.

Jason takes one last deep breath, centering himself, before answering. "Hey, Chuck."

"What's wrong, Jason?"

How the fuck does he always know?

"I'm just a little nervous, that's all."

Jason knows that's not the full truth, but he also doesn't feel like addressing the mild panic attack he just had.

"Oh, come on, bud, you've got nothing to worry about; you're going to do great," Chuck replies. "How is the team looking? And how have you been doing?"

"The team's actually looking pretty good," Jason says, responding quickly to avoid answering the second question.

"And what about you? How have you been doing?" Chuck says again, not letting him avoid the question.

Jason relents. "I'm okay, just sort of lonely at times, you know?"

"Have you tried connecting with anyone else who works at the university? I'm sure some of the other coaches would love to get to know you."

"No, not yet. Honestly, things have been so chaotic trying to get everyone on the team rowing in the same direction that I haven't had time to do much else outside of the job."

"That's okay, Jason. After all, it's still your first week. Brick by brick, right?"

"Very true," Jason responds. "I know I still haven't completely won over the team, but I'm actually getting to the point where I kind of miss being around them when practice is over . . . Is that weird?"

"Absolutely not, Jason. In fact, I'd say that means you care about them. And a coach who cares about their players is a coach who will do anything to help them succeed."

"Thank you, Chuck. You know, they're actually all out at one of the captain's houses tonight, having a team dinner."

"So, why aren't you there with them?"

"They said their team dinners were just for the players, and that the old coach never went to them . . . But part of me thinks they just didn't want me to come."

"Or maybe," Chuck counters, "they just don't feel comfortable enough around you yet."

"Let me guess, you think I should open up to them?"

"Well, it's hard to trust someone if you think they're holding back."

Jason knows he's right, but opening up has never been easy for him. Carrying the burdens of others always seemed like far less of a chore than letting someone help him carry his own.

"Maybe you're right, Chuck."

"Of course I'm right. I'm always right! That's why you keep calling me."

"Hey, you called me!"

"I know, I know." Chuck snickers. "Well, I should let you go; you've got a big day tomorrow. Good luck, Jason, and remember . . . never stop."

"Never stop," Jason replies, then hangs up the phone.

As he sits there, alone in his apartment, he takes a moment to recognize that he actually feels better. Chuck always has a way of making the impossible seem possible, of making the hardships in his life seem trivial. Jason's eyes drift around the room, eventually landing on his practice whistle that hangs rather elegantly from the key hook by his door. While his eyes remain planted on the cheap plastic device, his mind wanders . . . *I wonder how the team dinner is going?*

***

Jenny sits at the head of the table as the rest of the team funnels into the dining room of her small, one-bedroom apartment. Laid out in front of them are multiple large tin containers, filled to the brim with food that's emitting a heavenly aroma—even if it was purchased at a cheap local Italian restaurant. The fettuccine Alfredo sits in a bed of creamy melted cheese, and the garlic bread evokes a strange feeling of comfort and nostalgia when the scent hits her nose. "Alright, let's dig in!" she announces to the squad.

With that, twenty-two pairs of arms begin reaching over each other, and across the table, trying to grab everything they can.

"Hey, pass the salt, would you?"

"Whoa, this garlic bread is *fire*!"

"Game tomorrow, gotta carbo-load!"

All the voices around her form a fusion of sound as each player finishes filling their plate. What follows is the natural silence of a large group of famished people whose only goal is to stuff their faces with the delicious feast that lies before them. No one speaks for a short time, and the only sound that can be heard is the unmistakable chewing noise from everyone sitting around the table. After a few minutes, Jenny asks, "So, how are we all feeling about tomorrow?"

Her voice is commanding yet questioning; she has always felt herself to be the rock of this group, and she constantly feels the need to keep everyone on track.

"We haven't lost to those Brighton Banks Bastards before, and I don't think we will tomorrow, either," Dahlia boasts with conviction.

"Amen, girl," Dakotah says.

Daisy follows up quickly to complete the alliterative trio's praises: "Damn straight."

"You really are three peas in a pod, aren't you?" Jenny says, happy to see how the three of them act in such a united way.

Before they can respond, Sam speaks up: "It's not us I'm worried about . . ."

"Oh, not this again," Jenny fumes, knowing exactly what Sam is hinting at. "What is your big problem with the new coach?"

"*Coach?* Sorry, I'm not quite sure who you're referring to."

"Jesus Christ, Sam . . . Fine, what's your big problem with the *new guy* who tells us what to do at practice?"

"He's shit," Maddy replies.

"Yeah, total shit," Nicole adds.

"Can either of you think for yourselves?" Jenny barks back.

"Hey, we're just calling it like we see it," Nicole scoffs.

"Come on, Jenny, won't you at least agree he's a bit preachy?" Sam asks.

"What do you even mean by 'a bit preachy'?"

"Well, it's like every time he opens his mouth, he's telling us how we should act. Like he's almost talking down to us."

"Talking down to us? Sam, he's just trying to help us. Can't you see that?"

"Well, I don't need his help," Sam says, then turns her head away in defiance.

Jenny rolls her eyes before addressing the rest of the table, which has remained fairly quiet throughout this somewhat heated exchange. "Does anyone else have any thoughts about Coach Nash?"

No one says a word as each player looks to one another with slight concern on their faces, as if not wanting to speak up, for fear of disagreeing with either of their captains.

"I like him."

Jenny looks down the line of players to the far end of the table, and she's surprised to see that Luna was the one who spoke.

"What could you possibly like about him?" Sam chastises.

"He cares," she states, in an even-keeled tone.

"He cares? What the fuck does that even mean?" Sam replies.

"Listen, Coach Dickerson was fine and all, and I'm not saying he didn't care . . . But with Coach Nash, it just feels different. It's like he wants us to succeed for *ourselves*, not just for *the team*."

There's a brief pause, and Jenny can see Sam is contemplating the remark. Before she has a chance to rebut, Luna adds, "Chloe, what do you think? Didn't I see him talking to you this morning?"

Everyone at the table turns toward the now blushing Chloe.

"Y-yeah . . . he did help me," she stammers. "I was having a rough day, and he made me feel . . . I don't know . . . good. Like everything was going to be okay."

"Okay, so he helped a first-year find her confidence. Big whoop," Sam grunts back.

"What is your problem?" Jenny shouts, throwing her hands up in frustration.

"My proble—"

"He helped me too," Rachel interjects.

"What?" Sam replies.

"I was struggling with my on-the-run shot this morning before practice, and he helped me when I couldn't get it right."

"So, can we expect a perfect on-the-run shot from you in tomorrow's game?" Sam asks.

"Well . . . I haven't actually mastered it yet. But he just kinda helped me recognize that I should keep trying, and eventually, I can probably get it."

"Great. So he said some more preachy bullshit and made you feel good about yourself. Well, guess what—good feelings don't help us win games. When push comes to shove, the man just doesn't have what it takes to lead. He's got no bite."

"He does seem to know a lot about women's lacrosse, and he's good with a stick," Taya says.

"Yeah, come to think of it . . . How is he so good with a girl's stick?" Rachel adds.

"Who. The. Fuck. Cares," Sam responds, putting added emphasis on each word to drive her point home.

"Okay, enough," Jenny yells out across the table. "Why don't we wait until after his first game as our coach to judge him, okay? Because I'm willing to bet that he'll surprise us."

"Ha!" Sam scoffs. "I guess we'll see tomorrow, now won't we?"

CHAPTER 12

Jason's morning ritual on game days has always been the same. He wakes up early, straps on his running shoes, and goes for a three-mile run. Immediately after his run, he takes a cold shower to shock the body. Afterwards, he pours strong, medium roast coffee into a tall, chilled glass with ice and sits outside in the cool morning air while he enjoys it. When Jason finishes the coffee, he heads back inside to pick out the suit he plans on wearing for the game. In the past, people chastised his style choice, as they thought it was ridiculous for him to wear a suit on the sideline. They would say things like, "Lacrosse coaches aren't supposed to wear suits. Do you think you're better than everybody else?" or "You know this isn't basketball, right? You can just wear a school-branded sweatshirt or something." But the truth is, Jason doesn't wear suits because he wants to be different. He just likes looking good and professional. Suits always give him added confidence, and he refuses to let anyone else change that about him.

Today, the suit he chooses is a personal favorite of his. It's an all-black outfit from head to toe. He even makes sure to throw in a black pocket silk and a "Black Dahlia" lapel pin. *I bet Dahlia will like that,* he thinks as he pins the velvety artificial flower to his lapel. He completes his look with a pair of jet-black sunglasses and some freshly polished shoes that have been sitting in his closet for the past week, waiting for this day, just as he has.

As Jason goes to leave his apartment, he catches a glimpse of himself in the mirror hanging by his door. While he stares into the reflective rectangle that hangs on his wall, he takes a beat to reflect on everything that has led him here. Every small decision he made in his twenty-nine years of life that led to him standing here, in an apartment in Pittsburgh, Pennsylvania, about to go coach his first collegiate lacrosse game. Goosebumps pop up on his arms, and a chill runs down his spine as he takes a long, deep breath and smiles. *You got this, Jason . . . You got this.*

***

The lacrosse team is seated around the locker room, with no one really talking. Most of the players are wearing noise-canceling headphones and slightly bobbing their heads up and down to the music as they get in the zone before taking the field. Jenny isn't nervous per se, but she does feel a twinge of anxiety as she looks upon her fellow teammates. She respects her teammates, but they can be quick to judge, so today is the day that will truly set the tone for how they respond to the new coach moving forward. If things go well, the team can use the momentum to catapult past their deplorable start to the season. But if things go poorly, they may fall even deeper into the pit of failure in which they currently sit, to a point they can't come back from. This thought is making her very much on edge as she waits for Coach Nash to arrive.

We'd better win this fucking game.

Her eyes gravitate toward the clock on the wall; it reads 9:50 a.m. Coach Nash already told Jenny he'd be entering at 10 a.m., so she decides now is a good time to say a few words before he arrives. "Alright, ladies, headphones off." As she speaks, her teammates all do as they're told, then look back with anticipation about what she will say next. "I know we've had our troubles so far this year, but that doesn't mean we give up. Today, we play our game, and together, we can show them exactly who we are, and what it means to be a Blue Jay."

An array of responses shoots out from around her.

"Amen to that."

"Hell yeah!"

"Let's do this!"

These responses are quickly overshadowed by Sam proudly interjecting, "Nice speech, *Coach*."

Jenny shoots her a glare as the twins chuckle behind her. "Really, Sam? Sarcasm?"

"What? I'm paying you a compliment. I doubt the new guy's going to give a speech as good as that. Like I said last night . . . he's got no bite."

Right when Jenny goes to respond, the door whips open, and the room goes silent as they gaze upon the jet-black figure that stands in the doorway.

***

Jason stands in the threshold of the locker room and looks out upon his team. A small grin forms as he removes his sunglasses.

I guess they didn't expect the suit.

Before he has time to address the team, Taya yells out from the corner of the room, "Damn, Coach, that suit is *fresh!*"

Jason's grin grows into a smile as he enters the room. "Thank you, Taya." He waits a solid ten seconds before speaking again, making sure he has their full attention. "This week hasn't been easy, for you, or for me. Change is hard, and I'm not going to lie to you and tell you it isn't. But, ladies, as I look out upon this room, I don't see lacrosse players . . . I see warriors. Our backs are against the wall, and this is the moment where we either cower in fear, or we stand and fight, but that choice is yours."

"I'm ready to fight," Jenny states with pride, followed by a few more players chiming in from around the room.

"Those girls are trash."

"They don't stand a chance."

Jason waits for the murmuring to die down before he continues. "I know this team we're about to face may not be the most talented group of girls, but moving forward, I need you to understand something. Make no mistake, this season our goal is to bounce back and win it all. So, from now on, when we take the field, there are no more good teams or bad teams; all there are, are teams that are standing in our fucking way!" Jason's voice rises with ferocity and determination as he continues to shout. "This is where we fight! This is where we conquer! This is where we win, and this is where they lose!"

After Jason finishes, the room is electric. The mood has shifted from mildly motivated to downright ferocious. As the cheering fades, Jason adds one more comment before exiting the room. "Ladies, I dressed all in black today . . . like I was heading to a funeral. But let's make sure it's their funeral . . . and go bury this fucking team."

And with that, the room erupts, and Jason exits. As the team funnels out of the locker room and heads down *The March to Hell,* Jenny walks up to Sam and locks eyes with her. "How's that for some fucking bite?"

***

Fweet! Fweet! Fweeeeeeeet!

The final whistle blows, and Jason can't contain his elation.

"Let's goooo! Go get your goalie!" he screams as the entire sideline sprints onto the field and nearly tackles Chloe to the ground in excitement. Win or lose, it is always tradition to show your goalie love at the end of a lacrosse game, but it's certainly more fun when you get the win. As the team walks back toward the sideline, Jason can't take his eyes off the scoreboard. With a final score of 14–7, his new team gets its first win of the season, and he secures his first collegiate victory as well. The next ten minutes fly by in a blur as they all line up to shake the other team's hands. The endless echo of the players repeatedly saying, "Good game, good game, good game," rings out as the Blue Jays make their way down the line, shaking the opposing team's hands.

When Jason reaches the end of the line, he shakes hands with the opposing team's coach, telling them how great they played and thanking them for making the trip. Afterwards, he calls his team over to talk. While they all stand around him, he notes the joy that seems to be emanating from the players, which leads to a feeling of warmth and fulfillment that rolls over him.

"Ladies, I can't say enough how proud I am. You did an exceptional job playing *your* game, and the talent you possess really came to life out there on the field today. If we keep this up, the sky's the limit for this team, and no one will be able to stop us."

"Here, here!" Jenny chimes in, followed by a few more positive remarks.

"Hell yeah!"

"Ain't nobody going to get in our way!"

"Jays gotta fly!"

"There will be no practice tomorrow. Give your bodies some time to rest and recover from today, and then on Monday, we hit the ground running as we prepare for our next challenge." Jason looks at Jenny. "Captain, break 'em down."

"Alright, ladies, sticks up!" Jenny screams. "Jays on three—one, two, three, Jays!"

The chant ends, and the team exits the field, heading off to the locker room. At least ten or so players choose to approach Jason and thank him as they leave. *Well, that's more thank-yous than on the first day,* he thinks. *Brick by brick.*

While the team heads inside, Jason decides to stay at the field. He sits on the bench and watches as, one by one, every person in the stands leaves as well. After a while, it's just him, sitting there and smiling as he relives the last two hours in his mind. He wants to call Chuck, but he's fairly certain he'll have seen the score online and be calling him soon enough to congratulate him. So he just sits there instead, listening to the world around him. The wind is blowing, and the large American flag that stands at the far end of the field waves vigorously, making the rope attached to it start to sway. This creates a repetitive clanging sound as it whips against the pole that supports it.

Clang . . . clang . . . clang!

At first, Jason doesn't really notice it all that much, but as it continues, the sound persists until it's all he can hear.

Clang . . . clang . . . clang!

Clang . . . clang! CLANG!

CLANG! CLANG! CLANG!

Jason's vision goes white, and he suddenly feels faint. His ears begin to ring. A strong feeling of hopelessness washes over him as nausea kicks in, and he feels like he may pass out. He closes his eyes and clenches his fists as he begins to hyperventilate. Tears come without warning, rushing from his eyes like a faucet, as his body starts to shake. His mind races. *Why is this happening to me? What the fuck is going on? This can't be happening.*

He tries to talk himself down through the rapid breaths and fearful thoughts: "Breathe in, breathe out, breathe in, breathe out . . . Fuck!"

He screams into his hands as they cover his sobbing face. "Breathe in, breathe out, breathe in, breathe out."

Slowly, he can feel himself stop shaking, but his body remains cold and weak. A few more seconds pass. His ears stop ringing . . . He opens his eyes . . . He's all alone.

PART II

THE RED CARD

CHAPTER 13

Jason sits in his ergonomic chair, with his arms crossed in front of him, as his eyes fixate on the large, glossy whiteboard that is bolted to the office wall in front of him. A few weeks have passed, and he has been tracking the outcomes of every game he's coached so far. Being able to visually view and analyze how everything is going in a clear and concise manner has always helped Jason to keep his head in the game and remain focused.

Brighton Banks University - Score: 14–7 WIN (Non-Conference)

Shady Heights University - Score: 11–12 LOSS (Non-Conference)

South Bolton University - Score: 15–5 WIN (Non-Conference)

Glendale Hills University - Score: 9–2 WIN (Conference)

Overall Record: 3–4

As he looks over the scores, he thinks back to those games. After their first victory, the immediate loss to Shady Heights was a tough one. His team had fought hard for the full sixty minutes of gametime, but Shady Heights ended up scoring with only fifteen seconds left in the game to take the lead, and it simply wasn't enough time for his team to respond. Although this was a setback, Jason found solace in the fact that no one on the team let this loss deter their spirits. They showed up to practice the next day, kept working hard, and then came out the following week and put a beatdown on South Bolton University. And the conference win against Glendale Hills was the icing on the cake. Sure, they were by far the weakest team within their conference, but carrying the momentum of that win into the remaining eight games of conference play would be a huge motivator moving forward.

With all this good news, there was still one thing that continued to nag at him: the mental breakdown that occurred immediately following the Brighton Banks game. He had buried the experience deep within his brain. Every time the event popped back into his head, he pushed it back down and locked it away. It hadn't happened since, so Jason figured he shouldn't waste any time on it.

Why worry about the past? I should just focus on the future.

Even so, as he reviews the scores written on the whiteboard in front of him, the worry is still very much prevalent in his mind.

Vrr, vrr.

The sound of his phone vibrating on the table next to him breaks his trance; a quick look at the caller ID reveals that it's his mentor, Chuck, calling.

"Hey, Chuck!" Jason feigns excitement as he answers, trying his best to remove any distress from his voice.

"Jason, sorry it's been so long since we spoke last, but I wanted to call to say congrats! Winning three out of your first four games as coach is an incredible achievement!"

"Thanks, Chuck, that means a lot."

"Are you okay, Jason?"

"Yeah, I'm good, just a little tired, that's all," Jason responds, knowing it won't be enough to convince his mentor.

"Jason . . . I've heard you use the 'I'm tired' excuse far too many times for it to work on me anymore. So tell me, what's bothering you?"

"Well . . ."

"Is it the loss to Shady Heights? I know that was a tough one, but the team bounced back fairly well, so I wouldn't stay hung up on that! Plus, you got a huge conference win last week; only four more of those and you'll clinch a spot in the playoffs!"

Chuck's exuberance brings a little warmth to Jason as he sits in his swivel chair, using his feet to sway it from side to side.

"You're right, Chuck; it really has been a good few weeks. And I feel like I'm getting closer to winning over the entire team as well. There are still some holdouts, but it's progress. Brick by brick, right?"

"Yes, Jason, brick by brick. But . . . what else is bothering you?"

Jason weighs the decision to open up, and after a few seconds, he relents. He tells Chuck everything that happened after their first win. The happiness coursing through him as he sat alone on the bench reminiscing over their victory. The clanging of the flagpole that caused his brain to snap. The resulting panic attack that followed. He even tells him about how this event has troubled him ever since, popping into his mind every so often and reminding him that, at any moment, it could happen again.

"Jason . . . I'm so sorry you had to go through that. Panic attacks can be extremely scary, but why have you been holding on to this for so long? You should've called me."

"I don't know, I just . . . I didn't want to burden anyone else with my problems."

"Jason, that may be the dumbest thing I've ever heard you say."

"Excuse me? Chuck, I'm trying to be vulnerable here and—"

"No, Jason, vulnerability is asking for help when you need it. You have people who care about you and want to help you.

Jason, I know better than anyone the pain you carry every day; you have to let other people help you. Let us carry that burden with you."

Jason's eyes well up at the words from his mentor. "I know you're right . . . You're always right, Chuck," is all he can manage to say.

"Jason, I know I've brought this up before, but have you given any more consideration to talking with a specialist about this?"

Great, here comes the therapist talk again, Jason thinks, though deep down, he does feel an openness to the idea. Even after this small flash of vulnerability with his mentor, the weight on his shoulders seems a tad lighter. But he won't admit that to Chuck.

"I'll think about it, Chuck."

"That's all I'm asking, Jason. I care about you, and I just want what's best for you."

A tear rolls down Jason's cheek.

"I know you do, Chuck. I have to run, but I'll talk to you soon." Jason hesitates before adding, "I love you, Chuck. Thank you for always being there."

"I love you, too, Jason. Keep your head up, and please call me if you need anything."

The line goes dead, and Jason is left sitting in his chair, feeling both helpless and capable all at the same time. He's not sure what the future holds, but he knows he'll always have Chuck in his corner.

CHAPTER 14

"… Happy birthday to yoouuu!"

Jason and his sister are sitting at the kitchen table; a massive sheet cake lies before them with smooth vanilla icing and the words "Happy 16th Birthday" scribbled in red gel frosting across the center. The candles stuck into the cake all remain lit, the flames dancing in the air, waiting to be extinguished. Their mom and dad stand beside them with camera phones in hand, pointing them directly at their two little angels.

"Alright, kids, make a wish!" their mom emphatically announces, clearly for the benefit of the video she's taking, but still very much filled with excitement for her children.

Jason looks to his sister. "On three?"

"On three," she replies, and in unison, they both start to count.

"One . . . two . . . thre—"

Before they can finish saying *three*, his sister quickly blows out all the candles on the cake. She looks at Jason, whose mouth is now agape, and breaks out laughing. Jason gives her a playful shove and laughs alongside her.

"You better have made that wish worth it, since now I have to wait another whole year to get mine!"

"Oh, don't you worry, Jay. This wish was for the both of us."

"Oh yeah?"

"What did you wish for, sweetheart?" their mom asks.

"First, I wished for me and Jay to get recruited to our top schools for lacrosse; next, I wished for us to each score one hundred goals in our first year, and then I wished for us to win the Tewaaraton award as well; and then—"

"Whoa, honey! That's so many wishes; you only get one!" their mom interjects.

"Nuh-uh," she responds, shaking her head with a smile. "We're turning sixteen, so I get sixteen wishes!"

"Okay, okay, whatever you say, sweetie," their dad chimes in.

"Yup! Not that Jay and I need any luck to help us succeed. We are quite possibly the greatest lacrosse players in the world, and we're going to score so many times, and be together forever." She finishes speaking with a large grin on her face, and Jason throws two thumbs-up in agreement as their dad snaps a picture.

"Together forever," he repeats, "I like that."

"Sooo, who wants to open their presents?" their mom inquires, prompting both Jason and his sister to snap their heads in her direction like prairie dogs.

She gives a confirming nod, and they leap from their chairs and make their way into the living room to unwrap the gifts that are sprawled out onto the floor by the fireplace.

Fifteen minutes later, the floor is covered in crumpled wrapping paper, and an assortment of entertaining gifts lies in front of Jason and his sister. The clear winner was the Nerf Gun that they both received, as rubber darts are now scattered all around the room.

"So, kids, what do you think of your sixteenth birthday?" their mom asks.

"Amazing!" they both answer in unison.

"I'm glad to hear! But . . . I think there mayyyy be one last gift for both of you," she says.

"What?" Jason replies. "Where is it?"

"I don't know exactly, but you might want to check the backyard."

Both Jason and his sister jump to their feet and sprint to the back of their house. As they press their noses up against the window, their eyes land on a six-foot-by-six-foot orange lacrosse goal sitting in their backyard, the white netting attached offering a bright contrast to the green grass beneath it. Jason and his sister turn to each other with their eyes opened wide in astonishment.

"No way!" Jason yells as they both run out the backdoor toward their new gift, followed closely behind by their parents.

While they examine the brand-new lacrosse goal, every detail seemingly more impressive than the next to their sixteen-year-old brains, Jason turns to their parents, his face beaming. "Thank you so much! This is such a great gift!"

"Well, we figured it was about time we got you a real net, so you could stop using that ridiculous thing over there to shoot on," their mom replies, pointing her hand toward a six-foot-by-six-foot piece of mangled plywood that was leaning against their backyard chain-link fence. "So, do you want to try it out?"

"Yes! I'll go get the sticks. You gather the lacrosse balls," Jason's sister commands, and they both run off in different directions, a look of unwavering glee plastered on their faces.

"Hey, Jason . . . Jason? You okay?"

The sound of Lucy's voice snaps him out of his daydream. Jason is sitting inside The Iron Penn. In front of him stands an old-fashioned, made to perfection, the glass wet with condensation.

Jason grabs the cocktail and looks at Lucy. "Yeah, I'm good, just zoned out for a second, thinking about something I hadn't thought about in a while."

"Well, you looked happy, so I'm guessing it was a good memory?"

"Yes, it was . . ."

"So, hey, how come you didn't tell me you were the new women's lacrosse coach over at Crystal Summit?"

"Eh, honestly, I was so caught up with your amazing old-fashioned the last time I was here, I think it must've slipped my mind," he replies.

"Well, it looks like you've been doing well, so congrats on the great start."

"You'll have to come watch a game," he blurts out.

"You know what . . . Maybe I will," she says with a smile. "Just make sure you win if I do," she adds with a wink.

"Oh, don't you worry, with you as our good luck charm, I don't see how we could possibly lose," he responds, trying to keep up their innocent yet flirty banter.

"Oh, Jason, you're funny, you know that?"

As Jason sits there enjoying his drink, he can't seem to take his eyes off Lucy. He feels a connection with her. Unsure if it's the fact that he's still new to the area, and she's the only person he's really interacted with on a human level since he arrived; or if it's something else entirely . . . All he knows for certain is that he enjoys her company, and he wants to see more of her, whatever that may mean.

Jason finishes the last sip of his drink, then reaches into his pocket and pulls out some cash to drop on the bar. Before he can stand, Lucy approaches. "It was nice to see you again, Jason. Next time you come in, I want to hear more about this team of yours. Sound good?"

"It would be my pleasure," he replies with a smile.

CHAPTER 15

Jason can hear the sharp *crack* of lightning, and the long *rumble* of thunder that follows, from inside the athletes' lounge. He'd been tracking the storm since he woke up this morning. After realizing his hope that it would quickly pass them by was unlikely, he decided to cancel practice and call a team meeting instead.

When Jason first arrived at Crystal Summit about a month earlier, he had only peeked into the athletes' lounge during his welcome tour with Bill. Standing in it now, it appears far more lavish than he'd remembered. The sofas that line the walls are made of a fine, dark leather, and each cushion is embroidered with the school's Blue Jay mascot. The thin wall-to-wall carpet is well maintained and bears a black and blue checkered pattern throughout. And on the eastern wall is a seventy-five-inch flatscreen TV, mounted perfectly in its center.

At around five minutes to noon, the players begin to shuffle in, one by one, and take a seat to be ready for the meeting. They aren't very talkative this morning, which Jason hopes will keep the meeting on track. Jason looks at the clock; 11:59 a.m. His eyes scan the room, and he does a quick mental count.

Twenty-two, perfect.

"Alright, looks like everyone is here, so let's get started."

Before he continues, Jason notices something that he clocks as odd. Maddy and Nicole are sitting on opposite sides of the room, and from their body language, it seems like they aren't in the best of moods, but he chooses not to address it.

Probably nothing.

"Today, our main topic of conversation will be our next opponent, Emerald Hills."

A wave of sighs rolls over the room.

"I know, I know. I've looked over your history against this team, and it is true that in the past, you have left a lot to be desired when facing them."

"That's putting it lightly," Sam scoffs from the back of the room. "We straight up suck against them."

"Okay, yes. I may have been sugarcoating it. In fact, through your last five outings against them, they've outscored you 88–31. But I don't think that's any reason to not try."

"And just what the hell are you going to do to help us win?" Sam barks back, but this time sounding dismal and defeated.

I haven't seen this side of Sam yet, Jason thinks, and then responds, "One word: possession."

"Gee, never thought of that before," Maddy adds sarcastically, causing Jason to roll his eyes ever so slightly.

Without thinking, he looks over to Nicole on the other side of the room and waits for her to echo the sarcasm.

Nothing.

Huh . . . weird, he thinks, but he doesn't let it derail the conversation.

"Listen, the plan is simple. Emerald Hills has an absolutely explosive offense, so the best way to mitigate our risk is to keep the ball in our possession. That means, of the ninety-second shot clock we get, our goal should be to kill about eighty of those seconds before we make our move."

"Shit . . . that's actually not a terrible idea," Sam mutters under her breath, but Jason hears it.

"Thank you, Sam," he replies, feeling somewhat proud that he may have finally impressed a player who has shown him nothing but utter resentment since the day he arrived.

"It wasn't a compliment, just a statement of fact," she replies flatly.

Jason shakes his head. *There she is . . .*

The next thirty minutes are fairly productive as they discuss specific problems they've faced in the past against Emerald Hills, and also potential points of weakness they can exploit. Rachel suggests that they use the bounce shot technique, as they'll have a higher probability of scoring against Emerald Hills, since their goalie is strong in defending against high shots. Jenny suggests that they can work around Emerald Hills' aggressive defense by carefully timing their own passes, or throwing in some fakes, as this could potentially make them overcommit and leave players open. Overall, Jason is happy with how the meeting has gone. He dismisses them all and begins to pack up his belongings.

While the team is leaving the room, he hears Taya speak up. "Hey, Sam, what time should we be getting to your apartment for team dinner tonight?"

"We're supposed to get the food delivery at around 6 p.m., so anytime around then will work."

"Great, thanks!"

"Burgers and dogs for the *win!*" Dahlia shouts from behind her, and the rest of the team breaks out in laughter.

Jason hangs his head after hearing this. He knows they aren't used to having a coach at the team dinners, but it was something he truly enjoyed from his previous job. His subtle dejection is interrupted by a text from Bill:

Hey, Coach, I heard you're at the field house.
Swing by my office before you leave. Thanks.

Jason shrugs, then heads that way, locking the door behind him. When he arrives at Bill's office, the door is wide open, so he walks right in. Bill is in the middle of a phone conversation as he enters, so Jason stops in the doorway. Bill sees him and motions him in, mouthing the words, "It's okay, come in, come in."

Jason steps in and takes a seat in a powder blue chair, identical to the one he sat in on his first day visiting campus, the cold leather still offering comfort as it touches his skin. While he waits for the phone call to end, he looks around the room, taking in his surroundings. Atop the large wooden desk—that Jason guesses is probably made from oak or walnut—sits a large brass nameplate that reads "Bill Chapman—Director of Athletics." Next to it are a few stacks of paper, a monthly calendar with Bill's writing scrawled all over it, and a Pittsburgh Steelers bobblehead, which feels strangely out of place among everything else on the desk. Jason becomes so caught up in staring at the bobblehead, he almost doesn't hear Bill hang up the phone.

"Jason. Jason?"

"Hey! Sorry, I was distracted by your bobblehead," he replies, feeling no need to lie.

"Ah yes, my son gave me that. The kid is a huge Steelers fan."

"Oh, nice. So, is there anything in particular you wanted to talk about?"

"Yes. One of my contacts within our conference reached out because they heard Juliana Richards had entered the transfer portal," Bill responds, leading Jason to tilt his head and raise an eyebrow. He is certain he's heard that name before, but he can't quite place it.

"Okay . . . And should I know who that is?" Jason looks away, lost in thought. "Wait, she plays for Emerald Hills, right? I remember seeing her name on the scouting report."

"That's correct, and rumor has it, she may want to transfer here next season."

"Oh, really? Any reason why?"

"Apparently, she's unhappy with their nursing program, and I'm sure you've heard by now that our nursing program here at Crystal Summit is extraordinary."

"Oh yes, absolutely," Jason lies.

How the hell would I know that? I basically just got here.

"Well, she's strongly considering transferring here, and if she does, she would like to play for our lacrosse team. So, tomorrow, I want you to keep an eye on her and let me know what you think."

"Sure thing," Jason replies.

"Amazing! I know she'd be an incredible asset to the team next year."

"Was that all you wanted to discuss?"

"Yes, that was all. Feel free to reach out if you need anything, and good luck tomorrow! Let's go get that conference win!"

"Thank you, sir. I'll certainly do my best."

As Jason leaves the room, he takes a peek down the hallway that leads to the coaches' offices, and he notices someone standing right outside his, with their back to him.

"I wonder who that could be," Jason mumbles before he turns and walks in that direction.

Once he gets close enough, he recognizes her.

"Jenny?"

"Hey, Coach."

"You need something?" he replies, curious about why she's standing outside his office right after they just had a team meeting.

"Actually, yes. If you have a moment, I was hoping to ask for some advice. Is that okay?"

"Absolutely, come on in."

Jason unlocks the door, and they both enter. He plops down on his ergonomic desk chair and spins it toward her as she takes a seat on the small navy-blue couch that sits in the corner of his office.

"So, what can I help you with, Jenny?"

"Well, since I'll be graduating in a few short months, I was thinking about what comes next for me. I don't know if you're aware, but I'm a business major."

"I was not, but that is a fine career path," he replies, then suddenly realizes that he hasn't the slightest idea what any of his players are majoring in.

This disappoints him to some degree. Jason has always prided himself on his willingness and desire to get to know his players and show an interest in their lives. He felt it made for a better player-coach relationship, and it also helped with the teaching process.

"Well, the reason for me wanting to talk," Jenny continues, "is that I was debating starting my own business once I graduate."

"Oh, wow, that's amazing, Jenny. What kind of business are you going to start?"

"I was planning on opening up a bagel shop. A local store recently closed down in my hometown, and the space just went up for lease. So, I'm considering putting down a security deposit . . ."

Jason can hear the reservation in her voice.

"What makes you question the idea?"

"I mean, starting a business is risky . . . So many startups fail within the first year. It's kind of a scary thought, so I was hoping to get your input."

"Well, let me ask you this, Jenny. How long have you had this bagel shop idea?"

"Actually, since I was eight years old."

"Wait, really? You've had this idea for"—Jason does some mental math in his head—"fourteen years?"

"Yup!" she says, with a shimmer in her eyes. "I even have drawings of what I think the place should look like."

Jenny reaches into her bag and pulls out a large paper scroll. She unfurls it, revealing an in-depth drawing of her theoretical bagel shop. The detail she put into the drawing is incredible. Out front, there's a large sign with the name of the store, "BAGELS BY JENNY," in bold letters. Inside the shop, there are booths on both walls, with tables placed in the middle. Velvet ropes create an aisle between the tables for a line to form. These ropes lead straight to the large granite countertop, where customers will place their orders. She even drew a few employees standing behind the counter, all wearing matching green uniforms with name tags pinned at the top.

"Jenny, this is . . ." Jason finds himself at a loss for words as he tries to express his amazement with the drawing. "This is unbelievable."

"You really think so?" Her face lights up.

"I do. Jenny, this is clearly something that interests you, so if you want my honest advice. I say, go for it."

"If you really mean that, then I'll think about it."

Jason can tell she still has some reservations about the idea, so he adds, "Listen, I get it. Any big change in your life is going to be risky, and risk can be scary. The thought of not knowing what will happen next, and the constant fear of failure, can be terrifying. But, Jenny, if you never take a risk . . . years, even decades, can go by, and you may find yourself standing in the exact same place, having done nothing of value with your life, wishing you could go back. Without risk, you'll never grow, and if you're not growing . . . then what the hell are you doing?"

Jenny leans back, eyes wide in bewilderment. "Shit. That was kinda deep."

"I know, and I'm sorry. I don't mean to add any additional stress to your life; it's just . . . in my experience, when you take a risk and it ends up failing . . . the pain that failure creates is nothing compared to the regret you'd feel from never having tried in the first place."

"Damn . . . Well, you've given me a lot to think about. Thank you," she replies, then gets up to leave.

As she is reaching for the door handle, Jason stops her.

"Wait, real quick. What are your thoughts on Juliana Richards?"

"The attacker on Emerald Hills?"

"Yeah, her."

"Great lacrosse player; terrible person."

"Huh. Well, alright, then. Thanks, Jenny. Make sure to get some good rest tonight; we've got a big game tomorrow."

"You got it, Coach."

The door closes, and Jason is left alone with his thoughts.

Great lacrosse player; terrible person . . . I wonder what she means by that?

CHAPTER 16

As the sun sets over the horizon, Jason sits in his car, taking the time to reply to Chuck's *"Good luck tonight!"* text that he received just a few minutes ago.

When Bill informed Jason this morning that their Emerald Hills game had been moved from 11 a.m. to 6 p.m., he was excited at first—whether he was playing or coaching, he'd always loved games that took place under the lights. The enormous poles that supported the stadium lighting towered into the sky, and they offered full-field illumination that added a remarkable ambiance to the game. But the downside of having it moved to 6 p.m. was that it left Jason with seven additional hours to kill before game time. He's always felt some nerves before a game, which wasn't necessarily a bad thing. "It's just your body revving up and getting ready to take on a challenge," Chuck would tell him.

But this game in particular has a lot riding on it. It's a conference game, so the outcome will directly impact their chances of making the playoffs. Also, they'll be playing against a very talented opponent, so a victory would surely bring a hefty morale boost to his team—a loss, however, could send them into a spiral. To top it all off, Bill wants him to keep an eye on Juliana Richards—their star attacker—to see if she'd be a good addition to their roster next season. The whole thing had led Jason to feel incredibly on edge all day as he impatiently waited for 6 p.m. to arrive.

Sitting in his car now, he looks up at the digital clock displayed on the dashboard; it reads 4:37 p.m.

About ninety minutes to game time . . . I'd better head inside.

As Jason exits the car, he notices some people in the parking lot staring. Unsure about why he is attracting this seemingly undue attention, he shrugs and keeps walking until he sees his reflection in a nearby car door.

I guess a bright blue suit wasn't the most inconspicuous choice.

When he arrives in the field house lobby, Jason stops by a fountain to refill his water bottle, and he sees Chloe about ten feet away, talking with someone who he assumes is her dad. While he stands there, he can't help but eavesdrop on their conversation.

"You're gonna do great, honey. I know you are," the man says.

"Did Mom come?" Chloe replies.

So, I was right; this is her dad, Jason thinks.

"No, I'm sorry, sweetheart; she couldn't make it."

Chloe's shoulders begin to sag, and she drops her head.

"It's okay. She just needs a little more time, that's all. You know she still loves you, right?"

Chloe doesn't speak; she just looks down at the floor before giving him a hug, then heads down into the locker room.

"Huh . . . I wonder what that was about," Jason whispers under his breath.

Choosing to move past it, he heads in the same direction, making his way to the locker room as well.

As Jason opens the door, everyone stops talking. At this point, he's been their coach for long enough that they know he's going to give a speech when he arrives. Jason isn't about to let them down now.

"Alright, team, listen up. I've spent the past week trying to instill one thing in your minds . . . Forget the past. Emerald Hills has dominated this rivalry between us for the past five years, and make no mistake, they expect today to be no different. They think we've already lost, that the past defines us. So today isn't just about winning or competing . . . It's about whether they're right." At this point, Jason pauses, as he likes to do, hoping for some vocal input from the squad—and they do not disappoint.

"Oh yeahhhhh!"

"Woooooo!"

"Let's get it, baby. We got this!"

After a few seconds, Jason raises his hands to quiet the room. "That's right. So tonight, when we take that field, we live in *this* moment. For the next sixty minutes of gameplay, the past doesn't matter, and the future is irrelevant. For the next sixty minutes, it's just here and now; it's just us and them!" Jason's voice has risen to a thunderous volume as he continues, "Ladies, are you ready to fight?!"

"Yeah!" they all answer in unison.

"I hear you! Now make me believe you! Are you ready to fight?!"

"Yeah!" they scream, even louder than before.

"Alright! Now go out there, and show them who the fuck you are!"

***

When the opening whistle blows, Jason is begrudgingly surprised by how composed and put together Emerald Hills looks. They move together as a cohesive unit, each player seemingly knowing exactly where they should be at any given time. It isn't long before they draw first blood and score.

Unsurprisingly, it's Juliana Richards who scores first, performing an exceptional stutter-step rocker dodge to blow by her defender, Taya. She fakes high, and shoots low, placing the ball easily in the bottom corner of the net. As Jason watches the play unfold, he's genuinely impressed.

Maybe she would be a good addition to the team.

140

But as she drops her stick, instead of celebrating with her team, she proceeds to walk up behind Taya and mock her, screaming, "Woo! You like that?!"

Taya simply turns and walks away, so Juliana adds, "That's what I thought. I'll be here all night, ladies!" then dances away.

Jason is shocked by her behavior, and as he processes what just happened, he catches Jenny's eye on the field. She looks in his direction, then simply points her hand toward Juliana and tilts her head, as if to say, "See what I mean?"

Jason thinks back to their conversation from the day before. *"Great lacrosse player; terrible person." Yup,* he thinks, *she certainly wasn't wrong about that.*

***

Fweet! Fweet!

The referee blows the whistle to signify halftime, and Jason looks to the scoreboard. They're down 5–9 at the half, which is remarkable considering how poorly they've been playing. Juliana already has a hat trick, and after every goal she scores, she makes sure to mock her defender, letting them know exactly how badly they screwed up. Jason is baffled the referees haven't given her a yellow card for unsportsmanlike conduct at this point, but sometimes, the refs just let the players play.

On top of Juliana's dominance, the twins seem to be going out of their way to not include each other.

What a mess, he thinks, as both teams head to their respective locker rooms.

When Jason enters, it is anything but quiet.

"What the fuck are you all doing out there?!" Sam screams out, to no one in particular.

"Sam, we're trying our best, okay? Their defenders are talented. I don't know what else to say," Jenny responds.

"Trying? Trying won't get us into the playoffs, goddammit. You need to do better."

"Enough!" Jason shouts. "We only have ten minutes before we have to retake the field, so let's try and use that time wisely."

"Fine. Go ahead, *sir,*" Sam says flatly, adding an overt emphasis on the *sir* to make sure Jason understands he still hasn't earned the title of *Coach.*

"First up, Maddy and Nicole, what's going on out there? You've both had opportunities to feed each other the ball, yet you felt the need to make the selfish play and try to score yourself. Why?"

The room gets tense as Jason finishes speaking. Maddy is quick to respond. "We're *trying our best, okay.*"

As she says this, she looks at Jenny with a mocking glance, and rolls her eyes. Jason can tell Jenny is about to snap, so he takes over again.

"Maddy, stop. I'm done with the sarcasm. What's going on? You and Nicole usually work so well together, where is that twin sister telepathy we've seen before?"

This time, it's Nicole who fires back. "Hey, don't act like you know anything about what it means to be a twin."

Jason freezes, and an icy look crosses his face. His breathing becomes short and rapid, and he can feel his heartbeat accelerate rapidly. *Not the time,* he thinks, before taking a deep, expressive breath and replying, "Listen, it's simple. Start working together, or I'll find someone else who will."

"Yeah, okay. Sure you will," Maddy replies, clearly unaffected by what she seems to think is an idle threat.

"I'm not passing her the ball," adds Nicole.

"Good, I'm not either," Maddy says, then throws her sister a look of disgust.

"Jesus Christ! We do not have time for this!" Jason screams out to the room. "You know what. You're both done. I'm sitting you for the rest of the game, end of discussion."

Their faces go white with shock. This shock quickly turns to rage.

"Excuse me?" Nicole responds.

"The fuck you are?!" Maddy screams out.

"We're this team's best players. Without us, we won't win," Nicole adds.

"If you can't work together, you're hurting the team," Jason replies flatly.

"But—"

"This is not a debate. You're done."

Jason's voice is commanding enough to get both of them to relent, begrudgingly, and avert their gaze in frustration. The atmosphere becomes increasingly uncomfortable, and everyone in the room avoids making eye contact.

Jason glances down at his watch. "Fucking hell, we're down to five minutes before we retake the field. Okay, listen, to the offense, remember what we talked about—possess the ball, kill the clock, score the goal. And defense, that Juliana girl is rinsing us on attack, so Luna, I want you to faceguard her, okay?"

"What do you mean, faceguard?"

"I mean, wherever she goes, you go. I want you to be her shadow. Don't let her touch the ball," Jason replies bluntly.

"You got it, Coach."

Finally, someone who fucking listens.

"Everyone, I know that first half wasn't easy, but if we fall apart now, we might as well not even go back out there. So work hard and fight harder."

"Yes, Coach!" Jenny screams, trying her best not to sound deterred from any of the indecency that just occurred. "Sticks up, ladies," she says, and the team rises. "Jays on three—one, two, three, Jays!"

After the chant, they all quickly funnel out of the locker room. Jenny stops short as she approaches Jason.

"Bold move, Coach. I hope you know what you're doing."

"Jenny, sometimes it's important to send a message . . . even if it's not the most popular decision. Now go kick some ass."

"Yes, Coach," she replies, and they both exit the locker room to retake the field.

***

With only a minute remaining in the fourth quarter, miraculously Jason and his Blue Jays have cut the lead to one, with a score of 14–15. Luna has done an excellent job shutting down Juliana, who only scored one additional goal early in the third quarter, but has since been blanketed and unable to get involved in their offense.

Jason just called his final timeout of the game, and the plan he gave his team was simple: "Kill the clock so we can get the final shot of the game, score, and take this game into overtime." As the clock continues to tick away, Jason can feel his heartbeat speed up. They are moving the ball around quickly, and the Emerald Hills defense is desperately trying to keep up. As they struggle, the excitement builds inside Jason's chest.

Holy shit . . . We're gonna do it.

Seconds later, Jenny receives a pass and cocks back to shoot.

Fweet!

The whistle is sharp and fast, and it causes everyone on the field to stop dead in their tracks. The referee holds her hands above her head, with one placed in front of the other. "Shooting space," she announces, and the Blue Jays sideline lets out a loud cheer.

The announcer's voice booms over the loudspeaker: "It looks like the refs are saying the Emerald Hills defender was in the shooter's lane, so now, with only seconds remaining, Crystal Summit will have a chance to take an 8-meter shot on goal and equalize! I'll tell you what, folks, this is what college lacrosse is all about!"

As the referee places Jenny on the center hash of the 8-meter arc that fans out in front of the goal, Jason's palms begin to sweat. Jenny looks calm and collected as she stares forward at the eight meters of turf separating her from the goalie, who is planted in the center of the net like a tree, ready to make a save. Jason notices Taya on the far end of the 8-meter arc, seemingly uncovered by any defenders.

Will Jenny make the pass, or will she take the shot?

Making the extra pass might be the best option if they had more time, but time isn't a luxury they have at the moment. As the referee raises her hand before restarting play, Jason holds his breath.

Fweet!

The referee blows her whistle, and Jenny takes off. The next four seconds seem to happen in slow-motion. Jason watches as she takes a step off the line and looks toward Taya. She fakes the pass in her direction, in an effort to get the goalie to turn her head, but the goalie doesn't bite. Instead, she stands up straight, and as Jenny releases the shot, Jason already knows it won't find its mark. It's a well-placed shot, but the goalie tracks it perfectly and makes the save, leading to an uproar from the Emerald Hills sideline.

Fweet! Fweet! Fweeeeeeeet!

The final whistle sounds. The game is over.

The first ten to fifteen minutes after the game are dreary as they go through the motions. Before they head into the locker room, they shake hands with the other team, and Jason thanks the other coach for making the trip.

As he enters the locker room, the atmosphere is bleak. Some of the players have clearly been crying, but most of them are just sitting in their lockers, elbows resting on their knees, as they hang their heads in defeat.

Jason goes to speak, but Rachel beats him to it. "Ladies, I know that sucked . . . But honestly, I'm really proud of the way we played. We never gave up; we never stopped fighting, and we came closer than we've ever come to taking down Emerald Hills. We may not have gotten the win, but I still feel like a winner."

No one speaks for a few seconds, but she receives a few nods of agreement.

"Anyone else want to say anything?" Jason prompts.

"Luna did well," Chloe blurts out, and then her face quickly turns red, and she looks away.

"Agreed," says Jason.

"What about you, Coach? Do you have anything to add?" Jenny asks, her eyes puffy from crying.

"Nope." Jason looks at Rachel. "I couldn't have said it better myself. You all played your absolute hearts out, but sometimes . . . you just fall short. So, let's learn from it and move forward." Jason waits as the team accepts his words of encouragement, then says, "We've got tomorrow off, so take the time to rest up. Next week, I want everyone to stop by my office at some point so we can have mid-season meetings."

"Do we have to?" Sam says from the corner of the room.

"Yes, these are mandatory," Jason replies, and she doesn't fight him on it.

After the post-game meeting Jason ends up standing in the parking lot in front of the field house for a while after he leaves the building, trying to clear his head. The team is slowly exiting and finding their parents to chat about the game, and Jason is just staring up into the night sky, fixating on the stars twinkling above his head.

"What the hell were you thinking?!"

The loud, gruff voice snaps Jason out of his trance, and he looks to his right to see Jenny talking with an older man.

"I don't know, Dad. I thought I had the shot."

"You had your teammate wide open; you didn't need to take the risk! Make the easy choice, always."

"I know. I'm sorry. It won't happen again."

"It better not. I raised you better than that, Jenny. I'll see you next week."

He gives her a one-armed hug and abruptly walks away. When he does, she turns toward the field and gazes out over the turf.

All Jason can think is, *What an asshole,* before he decides to approach. "Hey, Jenny." She turns quickly and wipes a tear from her face.

"Oh, hey, Coach. Sorry, I got something in my eye."

"Are you okay?"

"Yes, I'm fine," she replies, then clears her throat. "And sorry about taking that shot. I should've passed it."

"Jenny, there's no need to apologize. Truthfully, I would've done the same thing. There just wasn't enough time for anything else."

Jenny smiles, then thanks Jason before leaving for the night. He heads back to his car. On his way there, he feels his phone vibrate inside his pocket.

When he removes it, Jason sees a text from Bill.

Hey, Coach, sorry about the loss. The girls played a heck of a game. But on the bright side, Juliana looked pretty good out there, am I right? She'll make a great addition to the team next year.

Jason thinks back on the game they just played. He recalls Juliana's reaction after each goal she scored: laughing in the face of her defenders, dancing and screaming like a lunatic, and mocking the players on the sideline. As Jason reflects on her performance, he shakes his head in disgust, and his mind goes red with indignation.

He types a short and concise text back, then puts the phone back in his pocket and heads home.

She's a liability. I don't want her.

CHAPTER 17

"Why the hell would you not want to add talent like Juliana to your roster?" Bill asks.

Jason had hoped that giving Bill the weekend to think it over would help him see it as he did, but clearly, as he sits in front of him now on Monday morning, he still doesn't get it.

"Bill, you hired me for a reason. On the first day we met, you told me this team was 'in shambles' and that they 'needed a culture change.' What message does it send if I bring in someone who thinks this kind of behavior is okay?"

Jason gestures toward Bill's computer screen where the highlights from their past game are playing on a loop, and the current clip shows Juliana dancing up and down the sideline as she hurls petty insults at their team.

"Jason, we need to win . . . And sometimes, that means making sacrif—"

"Not like this," Jason interrupts. "Listen, I understand that sacrifice is a part of success, but I've made progress with this team.

151

Not a ton, but enough. And adding this girl to our program would set us back to square one."

"Fine. If you don't want her, I'll let her know. But, Jason, we *do* need to win, so whatever culture change you've started, try to speed it up."

"I'll try," Jason says bluntly, then exits the room.

That was fairly painless, he thinks. *Now . . . time for some meetings.*

Jason's plan is to meet with every player on the team for their mid-season meetings today. He wants to get them all out of the way so he can focus on their next game, which will take place on Thursday of this week. Sam is the first to arrive.

"Hey," she says, entering the room, "let's make this quick. I've got class in an hour."

"Fine by me," he replies, fully expecting this meeting to be contentious, and not wanting to extend it any longer than it has to be. "How would you say things have been going?"

"Honestly, better than I would've guessed when I first met you."

"That's the closest I'll ever get to a compliment out of you, isn't it?" Jason replies, trying to add some levity to the conversation.

"Listen, benching the twins was a ballsy move. I'll give you that. But even a blind man could've seen they weren't playing well. I still think you've made some bad decisions. And I'm still not calling you *Coach*."

"You really have mastered the art of showing respect and disrespect all at the same time, haven't you?"

"What can I say? I'm gifted," she replies, and Jason can't say for sure, but he's almost certain he can see a thin, brief smile form on her face. "Are we done here?"

"Just one more thing. I should've brought this up sooner, but please try to go easier on Chloe, okay? It can't be easy stepping into her role as a first-year."

"The fuck does that mean?"

"Sam, at one point against Emerald Hills, you berated her for a solid thirty seconds after she got scored on from an 8-meter shot."

"So? I'm being a leader. Leaders hold people accountable."

"No, Sam, leaders lift people up when they fall. They don't kick them while they're down. She already feels the weight of this team on her shoulders, and when you berate her, that's just one more person telling her she's not good enough."

"Fine. Is that all?"

"That's all I've got; enjoy your class."

She gets up and leaves the room without a word.

Eh, that could've gone worse.

Just as Jason begins to feel confident this day will be a good one, Maddy arrives.

Earlier in the day, he had made sure to text both Maddy and Nicole separately to set up their meetings. If he was going to get to the bottom of what was going on between them, he needed them both in the room together, but he also knew they wouldn't want that. So, he sent them both the same meeting time of 10:15 a.m. As Maddy enters, Jason looks at his watch. It reads 10:11 a.m. *Just need to kill a few more minutes.*

"How are you doing today?" he asks, trying to get the conversation rolling.

"Pretty shitty. How 'bout you?"

Before Jason can address the hostile response, Nicole walks in.

"Oh, for fuck's sake. What the hell is she doing here?" Maddy says as she enters.

"Nicole, have a seat." Jason does his best to sound calm and composed as he speaks.

"Why. Is. She. Here?" Maddy asks again, pointing toward Nicole.

"Okay, listen, I can see you're both still a bit heated from the game, but I needed you both here because I need to know what is going on between you two. You said it yourself, you're the best players I have, but if you can't work together, you'll be spending a lot more time sitting on the bench. Understand?"

Both Maddy and Nicole look at each other with disdain. Jason can sense the palpable tension in the room as they consider what he said.

"No. I can't do this," Nicole says bluntly, then walks out.

She leaves so quickly Jason doesn't even have time to stop her. He looks to the ceiling in frustration and whispers under his breath, "Goddammit . . ."

While staring up at the stark white popcorn ceiling, he hears a whimper. When he looks back down at Maddy, she has tears in her eyes. "Maddy? What's wrong?"

"N-nothing, I'm fine; leave me alone. You wouldn't understand," she stammers, trying to stifle her tears.

"Maddy . . . it's okay," Jason says, in a soft, nurturing way, as he slowly closes the door to his office. "What's wrong?"

She looks away from him and hesitates to speak as tears now stream down her face.

"It's Nicole," she blurts out. "She wants to transfer to a different school next year. She says she wants to go to California to *try something new*."

"Okay . . ." Jason says, unsure why this would cause her to break down in the manner she has. "So, what's the probl—"

"She's abandoning me!"

"Shit," Jason whispers to himself.

Suddenly, he understands.

"She's abandoning me, and she didn't even talk to me about it! I found the stupid letter in her trash from a school in California asking her to come visit . . . She wants to leave me!"

The tears have turned into a waterfall as the emotion takes over her body, and she struggles to catch her breath from yelling.

"Maddy . . . have you spoken to Nicole about this?"

"Of course I have! I found the letter and immediately confronted her!"

"Okay, but Maddy, have you spoken to Nicole about . . . *this*." He gestures toward her as he speaks, emphasizing the emotion that is pouring out of her. "If she doesn't know why you're upset with her, it may be hard for her to understand your anger."

Her sobbing fades, but she continues to sniffle as she wipes the tears off her cheeks. "W-what do you mean?"

"I mean, it sounds to me like you found the letter, and then just lost your cool and yelled at her. But since then, have you expressed any emotions besides this dismissive anger? Have you had a *real* conversation where you told her how you feel?"

"No . . . I guess not. I yelled at her, and then she yelled back; and then we just kind of avoided each other . . . But I doubt she would even understand."

"I think you should give your relationship more credit. I've watched you both, and I can see the love you have for each other. Siblings share a kinship unlike anything else, and right now, she knows you're mad, but she doesn't know why. Tell her why."

Jason can feel himself getting a little choked up by the conversation as he waits for her to respond.

"Maybe," she says, sniffling. "I'll think about it."

"Okay, that's all I'm asking. And if you need anything, let me know."

"Yup. Will do. I have to go."

Maddy stands up abruptly and exits the room with haste. Now that he's alone, Jason rubs his brow aggressively and looks at the team roster on his desk. He crosses off the names *Sam*, *Maddy*, and *Nicole* from the list.

"Three down, nineteen to go. Holy shit . . . Why'd I think I could do this all in one day?"

The next eighteen meetings go by fairly painlessly. Most of the team has good things to say, and they offer some decent opinions on how to improve the team. Rachel mentions that she's continuing to work on her on-the-run shot, and she feels like she is nearly there. Daisy, Dahlia, and Dakotah all come in one after another, with nothing but positive things to say. Jason has begun to enjoy their upbeat attitude more and more as he gets to know them. As the hours roll by, everyone comes and goes until there is only one person remaining, Chloe.

Knock, knock.

She opens the door and peers around the corner.

"Hey, Coach, can I come in?"

"Yes, come in, Chloe; have a seat," Jason replies. "How are you doing today?"

"I'm fine," she says flatly, but Jason picks up a subtle hint of despondency.

"Just fine?"

"I mean . . . school's going okay, but I've got a big test next week that I'm worried about. Also, I'm still kinda bummed about the game this past weekend."

As Jason listens, he can see she's struggling to make eye contact with him, and he gets the sense she may still be holding something back.

"Is that all?" he asks.

"Um, yeah . . ." she replies, still averting her gaze.

Jason doesn't want to pry, but he's also fairly sure he's right, so he makes one final attempt.

"Chloe, you know these meetings are confidential, right?"

She finally meets his eyeline, and he can see her thinking it over.

"There is something else, I guess . . . My girlfriend and I just broke up."

"Oh, damn, that sucks. I'm so sorry, Chloe."

"Thank you, but honestly, that's not what's on my mind. I was actually the one to end things between us."

"Oh?" he offers, allowing her to elaborate.

"Well, we were good together, but the spark had kinda gone out, you know? And also . . . well, there's someone else."

Jason absorbs the new information.

Why would she confide in me about this?

After a moment, he begins to piece it together, and it clicks. "It's someone on the team, isn't it?"

"Yes . . . It's Luna," she replies.

"Oh, well, that's great," he says, unsure how to react. Even as he responds, he realizes how unequipped and out of place he feels offering her advice on the matter. "So, what's the dilemma?"

"I want to tell her how I feel, but what if she doesn't feel the same way? Or what if . . . I mean . . . I know she's dated women before, but what if she doesn't like me back?"

"Chloe. I'm not going to lie and tell you I'm at all qualified to give advice here . . . but do you remember what I told you a few weeks ago at practice?"

She tilts her head in thought.

"I told you that there's something scarier than putting yourself out there and failing . . . And that's never getting the chance to try. Sometimes you have to put yourself out there and hope for the best; sometimes . . . you have to take the leap."

"But what if she doesn't feel the same way?"

"Then you'll know, and you can move on. That's how life works, Chloe."

She looks at Jason with uncertain eyes before replying, "You're probably right. I'll think about it . . . Thanks for listening."

Jason has a strange feeling she's still holding something back, but he doesn't want to pry any further.

"My pleasure," he replies, and she stands and exits, leaving Jason alone to reflect on the conversation.

CHAPTER 18

"Oh, my God! Oh, my God! Oh, my God! It's them! They're calling!" Jason's sister screamed as she stood in front of him, shaking with excitement, while looking down at her phone.

It was the summer before their senior year of high school, and they were preparing to leave for a lacrosse tournament located in Northern New Jersey. A few weeks prior, Jason had received a similar call to the one his sister was receiving now. Jason's call had been from Syracuse University. They were his number one choice for both academics and lacrosse; and the head coach of the program called him directly and offered him a spot on their roster. The feeling of pure elation that flowed through his body when he got the call was electric, but it was nowhere near as amazing as the feeling he got when his sister had found out.

After that call, she screamed, "Oh, my God, you did it, Jay!" and then leaped toward him and tackled him onto the couch with an enormous hug of excitement, leading them both to roll off onto the floor, laughing hysterically.

Unlike her brother's important call, it was not someone from Syracuse waiting on the line for her; it was someone from Northwestern. This was her number one choice of colleges, and on the other end of the phone call was the head coach of their program. While it did make Jason sad thinking of his sister going to a college eleven hours away from him, they had both talked about it a lot in the previous months, and they planned to visit each other as often as possible, if they could.

"We're also going to talk every day, and you're going to help me with my math homework, because math is stupid, and you're good at it," she had told him, cackling while she spoke. When Jason had still seemed down, she added, "Eleven hours is nothing. We'll be together forever!"

"Well, go ahead! Answer it!" Jason said to his sister.

"Okay, okay, here I go!" she replied, then answered the phone.

Jason couldn't hear the coach on the other end of the call, but as he listened to the muffled voice emanating from the phone speaker and watched the small grin on his sister's face grow into an ear-to-ear smile, he knew she'd been offered a roster spot as well.

"Thank you so much! I'd love to play for Northwestern. I really appreciate the call. I can't wait!" she said, her face still beaming.

After a few more minutes of talking, she ended the call.

"You did it!" Jason screamed.

"*We* did it!" she said. "I wouldn't be here if you hadn't helped me get better every step along the way."

"And neither would I," he replied.

"Ahhh! I'm so excited! How should we celebrate?"

"We're about to leave for a lacrosse tournament," Jason reminded her.

"Oh, right! Ha! I'd forgotten. I can't think straight. My mind is buzzing!"

"I'm so happy for you, Sis," he replied, giving her a massive hug.

Right as they pulled apart, their parents hustled into the room.

"What is all the commotion in here? We heard yelling," their mom asked.

"Mom! Guess what!" she replied, completely disregarding the worry in her mom's voice.

"What, sweetheart?"

"I got accepted!"

"Northwestern?" her dad asked.

"Yes!" She could barely contain her emotion. "I'm going to be a Wildcat!"

"That is amazing, honey. I'm so happy for you! I can't wait to hear more about it, but you three should be leaving, don't you think?"

Their mom looked at the clock on the wall.

"Oh, wow, look at the time. Yes, we should get on the road."

"Are you sure you can't come, Dad?" Jason asked.

"Oh, buddy, you know I've got this work conference in Chicago. But you call me after every game to tell me how they went, okay?"

"Will do!"

"Now, go help your sister load the car, okay?"

"Okay." Jason picks up his lacrosse bag and looks to his sister. "Race you to the car?"

"You're on, Jay. On three?"

"On three," Jason agrees, "One, two, thr—"

Halfway through the word "three" he takes off sprinting.

"Hey! Not fair!" she yelled after him, chasing him out the door and laughing all the way.

Shortly thereafter, they finished loading the car, and their mom set the GPS to their New Jersey destination. Jason glanced at his sister as she gazed out the window with a giddy smile on her face, her innocent eyes looking off into the morning sky. She slowly turned her head toward him and met his gaze. As they stared into each other's eyes, Jason felt a sense of overwhelming warmth and joy. He couldn't remember the last time he'd felt so content and carefree, with the whole world ahead of them. Right as their mom put the car into gear and pulled out of the driveway, his sister mouthed to him the words, "We did it."

"Jason? Jason? Are you there?" Chuck said into the phone, his voice snapping Jason back to the present.

"Uh, y-yeah, I'm here, Chuck. Sorry about that. What did you ask?"

"I asked how you're feeling about today's game. I know your loss against Emerald Hills was a tough one, but this is a good opportunity to bounce back!"

"I'm feeling okay. Sorry, I've just got a lot on my mind," Jason replies.

"Anything you want to talk about?"

Jason thinks back to everything that's happened in the last few days: the meetings with his players, the contention between Maddy and Nicole, his conversation with Chloe, and even the memory he was just thinking about that is still prominently fixed at the center of his brain.

"Honestly, not really," he replies, hoping Chuck doesn't prod any further.

"Okay, well, I'm always here if you want to talk," he says. "Good luck today. I know you're going to do great."

The line goes dead, leaving Jason alone again, with nothing but his thoughts to comfort him while he sits in his apartment, sipping the large, iced coffee in front of him.

CHAPTER 19

Jason's drive into campus is just like any other day. It takes him roughly twelve minutes to get from his apartment to the field house, and he spends every second of those twelve minutes thinking about the game he's about to coach. With seven conference games remaining, they will have to win at least four of them to be guaranteed a spot in the playoffs. It doesn't seem like it would be that challenging a feat to overcome, but Jason knows better than most that you never know what life is going to throw at you. As he drives along the back roads leading to the field house, he finds himself once again rubbing the water lily tattoo on his wrist, a telltale sign he might be a bit more stressed than he's letting on.

The opponent for today's matchup is a well-renowned team in their conference, the Prescott Ridge University Grizzly Bears. Jason doesn't know much about them, other than what he learned from the film he watched, but Bill had warned him earlier in the week that their fans can get extremely rowdy. At the time, he thought, *How bad can they be?* But as he pulls into the parking lot now, the picture becomes clear.

The lot is nearly full, and the away fans have walled off their own little section to tailgate. Nearly all of them are sporting the red and black signature colors of Prescott Ridge, and many have chosen to paint their faces in the same manner. As Jason gets closer, his nose is bombarded with the smell of charcoal grills and barbecued meats, and his ears get wrecked from the sound of unintelligible screaming coming from the mob of fans. Jason can feel his chest getting tight as his body experiences a sensory overload, so he speeds past the crowd to the end of the lot where he finds an open spot to park.

Once inside the building, he can sense the beady eyes of everyone around him staring in his direction. He knows the three-piece suit is probably a tad much, but subtlety has never been one of his strong suits. When he approaches the locker room, he can hear rap music blaring from within.

At least they're getting hyped up.

When he enters, Jenny is quick to notice him and kills the music.

"How are we feeling?" Jason asks nonchalantly.

"Pissed off about Emerald Hills and ready to fuck shit up," Sam shouts from the corner.

"Alright!" Jason says. "Now that's some top-tier energy right there."

"Yeah, these bitches 'bout to get cooked!" Maddy shouts.

"Oh shit! That's what I'm talking about!" Jason responds, truly loving the atmosphere in the room. "Well, listen, I'll make this short and sweet. Today is a big game, and it will by no means be easy. But great people don't do great things because they're easy . . . Great people do great things to prove how great they are!"

In response, the team fills the room with loud and rambunctious cheering.

"Let's goooo!"

"This is our game!"

"Woo! We got this!"

"Alright, ladies! Let's go out there and show them just how big of a mistake it was, thinking they could walk into our house and leave unscathed!" Jason adds as he opens the door to the locker room, handing out fist bumps to everyone who is willing as they pass.

Once the room is clear, he closes the door behind him, shuts his eyes, and then just stands there and listens. The only sound he can hear is the roaring of the players gradually fading as they get farther and farther down *The March to Hell*. Jason takes a deep breath and opens his eyes.

"Here we go . . ." he says to himself, then makes the long trek down the hallway, through the double doors, and onto the battlefield.

***

Ten minutes into the second quarter, things are going fairly well with the score at 10–8. They have managed to hold on to this two-goal lead for the entire quarter, but they can't seem to pull away. Every time they score, Prescott Ridge answers back with a goal of their own. While this isn't ideal, what Jason finds far more irritating is the relentless heckling coming from the opposing team's fans. They're close enough to his sideline that he can hear almost every insult, slander, and taunt thrown his way: "Jackass!" "Loser!" "Dipshit!" Jason's heard it all before, and he usually doesn't let it bother him, but as the barrage of hate continues, he feels himself getting exceedingly more on edge.

As the last minute of the quarter is winding down, a player from Prescott Ridge commits what Jason believes to be an illegal check, basically shoving Daisy to the ground and causing her to let out a nasty scream. Jason looks to the referee for a call, but gets nothing. Even though he knows a ref will seldom change their mind, he decides to offer his opinion anyway.

"Ref! Are you out of your mind? How are you not going to call that?"

"Ohhh, poor baby didn't like the call?" a voice yells out from behind him.

Jason turns to see a scrawny, bald man, who's now pointing and laughing at him. He tries his best not to engage with the opposing fan.

No need to escalate things.

"What? Nothing to say?" the man screams out, begging Jason to respond.

It's not worth it, Jason. It's not worth it; it's not worth it.

The final seconds of the quarter tick away, and the score remains the same at 10–8 as both teams exit the field and head toward the field house doors to get to their locker rooms. Jenny leads the pack while Jason brings up the rear as they make their way inside, and he is almost to the double doors of the field house when he hears it. A comment that cuts through all the noise.

"Yeah, keep walking your dumbass off the field in that pretty boy suit," the man yells.

Jason stops for a moment and shakes his head, but as he goes to keep walking, the man adds, "You got real *'only-child'* energy, you know that?"

Jason freezes. A sharp pang of tinnitus rattles in his eardrums. His heart begins pounding in his chest. He can feel his adrenaline spike as his face goes pale, and his mind goes red.

In the coming days, Jason will hear multiple different accounts of exactly what happened during this event. How he froze in place and his face washed over with rage. How he jumped the four-foot fence that separated the field from the stands, then sprinted toward the man with fury in his eyes. How his players were screaming to him from behind the fence: "Coach! Coach! Stop!" But no words were getting through.

Every eyewitness account will help him better understand why he received a three-game suspension for his actions. But all he'll be able to remember from this day is coming to, mid-rant, screaming into the face of the scrawny, bald man—completely unaware of how things had escalated to this point, and unable to stop.

"How about you say that to my fucking face!" Jason hollers, spittle flying from his mouth. He can feel the veins in his forehead pulsating.

"What? Nothing to say now, you whack bitch!"

An arm wraps around Jason's body, and he snaps his head to his right. Bill is standing by his side, trying his best to separate Jason from the man.

"Jason! You have to stop! Jason!" he pleads, struggling to pull him away.

Jason's mind starts to calm a bit. He takes a few steps back and looks around. Everyone in the stands looks terrified, standing motionless like statues, their faces white with fear. He's having trouble catching his breath, and he can already feel the fatigue setting in as his adrenaline wears off.

Bill grabs him by the shoulders. "You need to go inside—right now!" he orders. "I'll handle this."

Jason does as he's told. On his way inside, he passes right by the referee. She is blowing her whistle frantically and holding up a red card at Jason. He pays her no mind as he walks past her and goes through the double doors.

Every step he takes down the long hallway makes the pit in his stomach sink deeper. His eyes stare aimlessly down at the floor in front of him as he walks. Before he knows it, he's in front of the locker room door. He takes a deep breath and opens it.

The energy inside the room changes from muffled confusion to dead silence as the hinges swing open. Jason slowly walks to the front of the room and leans back against the wall. His eyes are still empty wells of nothing as he looks toward the ground, unable to make eye contact with his team. No one makes a sound; they're afraid to say a word. They all just sit there in their lockers, until finally, someone speaks up.

"Dude . . . what the hell was that?"

Jason looks up to see Sam staring back at him. He goes to open his mouth, but nothing comes out, so she continues speaking. "All the guy did was make fun of your suit, and then say you had 'only-child energy.' I mean, for God's sake, I've said worse things to you than that."

There is a long pause before Jason responds. "I know I owe you all an explanation . . ." he says, his eyes welling up. It's clear from their expressions that he's piqued their curiosity, but they all remain quiet and lean in.

"I used to have a sister."

With those six simple words, Jason can see the players' eyes grow wide as they glance at each other and exchange looks.

"I used to have a sister . . . And we did everything together. One day—"

Jason stops to sniffle, struggling to go on.

"One day, we were heading to a lacrosse tournament. My mom was changing the radio station, and we were in the backseat, joking around without a care . . . when, out of nowhere, an SUV ran a red light and crashed into us."

The players let out subtle gasps, but no one speaks, and Jason remains motionless.

"It all happened so fast . . . I ended up walking away unharmed, with nothing but a few scrapes and bruises. But my sister . . ."

Jason stops. His throat swells, and his vocal cords get tighter. Tears that had been welling up in his eyes gently glide down his face.

"My sister died on impact. One minute, she was sitting beside me in the back seat, laughing and smiling with the whole world ahead of her . . . And the next minute, she was gone . . . And it broke me."

At that moment, it feels like his heart's in his throat as he struggles to swallow. He puts his hands to his face in a desperate attempt to hold back the tears.

"She was my other half . . . She was my rock . . . She was my best friend . . . And I—"

Jason starts sobbing, completely giving in to his emotions.

"I miss her so much right now." Jason stops again, barely able to get the words out. "I just really wish she were here."

When he finishes speaking, there is a lull, and Jason looks around the room. Some of the players have tears in their eyes. Others are just sitting there with blank expressions. When his gaze falls on the twins, he can see Nicole has reached out and is holding Maddy's hand—through tear-filled blinks, he sees her mouth the words, "I'm sorry."

Jason is torn. It feels good to get this off his chest, but now, he's unsure where to go from here. Just as his emotions peak, and it all becomes too much for him to bear, Sam stands and walks toward him in stride.

"Sam, please . . . I just can't right now—" he chokes out, but before he can finish, she wraps her arms around him and squeezes him tight.

Jason isn't sure what to do. His arms slowly complete the hug, and for a few seconds, they just stand there in the front of the team, as if no one is watching. Eventually, Sam pulls away, but she keeps her hands on his shoulders as she looks into his eyes.

"Loss is hard."

"I know . . . And listen, I'm sorry about the red card . . . I know I let you all down—"

"Stop," Sam interjects. "You didn't let anyone down; as far as I can tell, that asshole had it coming."

A small grin appears on Jason's face as he wipes a tear from his cheek. It's strange seeing Sam so supportive, but he isn't about to question it.

"Can I ask you something?"

Jason just looks at her and nods.

"Your sister—what was her name?"

Jason swallows, and his eyes glance down at his wrist. He sniffles before looking back into her eyes. "Lilly," he replies as more tears cascade down his face, and he averts his gaze.

"Hey, look at me. If you need anything"—Sam gestures her hand around the room—"we're here for you. All of us. This is your family now."

Jason looks around the room and smiles through stifled sobs. He's a bit too choked up to speak, so he mouths the words, "Thank you."

"And as for the game"—Sam gestures toward the team again —"we got this . . . Coach."

At her use of the word *coach*, Jason's eyes light up and lock onto hers. Tears are still falling down his cheeks, but a smile has formed on his face. As he looks around the room, Jason realizes how lucky he is to be here. He may have lost his family, but today, he gained a new one.

CHAPTER 20

"Take a look at that!" Sam yells as she slams a newspaper down on the table in front of Jason.

A day has passed since the game against Prescott Ridge, and the team has gathered at Jenny's apartment. Jason grabs the newspaper and examines it. On the front page is a photo of him that someone took during the sideline ordeal. He is standing in front of the man, mid-scream, with his finger pointed toward him in a threatening manner. He then sees the headline: "Head Coach Goes Ballistic."

"Ha!" Jason chuckles. "You know, that's actually not a bad photo of me."

The team breaks out in laughter, and Jason continues to read the article out loud.

"Although Crystal Summit came out of the locker room having to weather the storm of a five-minute red card penalty—brought on by their head coach, Jason Nash—the team didn't crumble; instead, they appeared to rally behind his rage."

"Yeah, we did!" Nicole says.

"Hell yeah!" Maddy adds.

Jason smiles. *It's nice to have them back on the same page.*

"Honestly, I just want to say again how proud I am," Jason replies, addressing everyone at the table. "You ladies came out of that locker room and showed the world what true resilience looks like. I'm not sure there are many other teams that could've persevered and won the game like you did."

"You taught us how to fight back," Rachel responds.

"But I also taught you to control your emotions . . . which I definitely failed to do. So again, I'm sorry about that."

"Don't sweat it, Coach," Sam adds. "As you were screaming in the face of that asshole, I kept thinking to myself, *This might be the most I've ever respected you.*"

Jason laughs. "You know, it's still weird hearing you call me coach."

"Eh, it feels weird coming out of my mouth too, but I'd say you earned it. Did I hear you call that guy a *'whack bitch'*?"

The team erupts in laughter, and Jason tries not to spit out the drink he just took a sip of.

"That I did," he replies with a smile. "Not my proudest moment, but he did have it coming."

"Hey, Coach, is it too much to ask you more about your sister?" Jenny says from the head of the table.

"Not at all, Jenny. Ask me anything you want."

"Well, what was she like?"

Jason looks down at the table, remembering back to when they were younger and doing his best to maintain level emotions.

"She was . . . the best sister anyone could ask for," he says, then looks at Maddy and Nicole. "No offence, ladies."

"None taken," they reply in unison.

"She loved to joke around, and she never took anything in life too seriously. She believed that life was too short to waste it being angry."

Jason feels his lip start to quiver.

"Did she play lacrosse too?" Dahlia asks.

"She did. We used to play around every day in our backyard."

"Wait, so, is that how you know so much about women's lacrosse, and why you're good with a girl's stick?" Rachel asks.

"Yup, I went to every one of her games—and whenever we'd get bored playing in the backyard, we'd swap sticks to mix things up, and see who was better."

"Hold on!" Sam cuts in, "So, you fucking hustled me?! At that game of Horse?"

"Yes, I did." Jason laughs. "Sorry about that. Lilly and I would play outside for hours at a time, just trying to get better. We even made up our own trick play."

"Trick play? What was it?" Jenny replies.

"It's a play designed for when the opposing defense is in an all-out press and playing aggressively. Basically, a midfielder positioned up top gradually inches backward toward the thirty-yard restraining line, and once she gets close enough, she simply steps backward over it. At which point, the defender on the opposite side of the field steps over into the offensive zone, then takes off running, to create a fast-break opportunity."

Jason can see everyone at the table trying to visualize the play as he's described it.

"Fuck . . . that actually might work," Jenny finally replies. "What did you call it?"

"You know, we actually never gave it a name."

"Huh, well, I like it," she says. "Tell us something else about her."

"Well, she was committed to Northwestern to play lacrosse."

"Wait, for real?" Rachel chimes back in. "So, she must've been *really* good."

"Yes, she was. Top scorer on her high school team three years in a row," Jason boasts.

"Did you play lacrosse in college?" Sam asks.

"I committed to Syracuse."

"Wait, what? How the fuck did we not know that?"

"You never asked," he says with a shrug. "But I should also mention that I never actually played a single game for them."

The players look at him with puzzled faces, so he elaborates, "After the accident, things got rough, and I didn't cope well. In my first month at school, I got into three fights and was kicked off the lacrosse team. I would've been expelled had an old mentor of mine not reached out and helped me get my life back on track."

"Shit . . . Coach." Sam looks at him with sorrow in her eyes, then says, "I gotta say, I'm sorry for being such a dick this year. How did you not lose your absolute shit on me every single day?"

"It's okay, Sam, you didn't know," he replies softly. "And yoga helped," he adds, attempting to pump some levity into the conversation.

"Wait, Coach . . . There's something I don't understand. Who was this mentor that helped you, and why wasn't it your parents?" Rachel inquires.

Jason's face goes dim, and his eyes gloss over as all emotion seems to escape him.

"After the crash, my mom had to undergo emergency surgery, and complications led to her losing a leg. The doctors prescribed meds for the pain that she eventually got hooked on. She turned to booze as well to cope with the whole situation, and let's just say . . . We don't talk much anymore."

Twenty-two pairs of wide, unblinking eyes stare back at him until Sam finally utters the only thing that comes to mind: "Fuck . . ."

"Yeah, pretty shitty, right?"

"And what about your dad?" Rachel asks.

"My dad . . . well, he just up and left. He walked out and never looked back. He gave up on his family. He abandoned us."

Rachel's eyelids begin to droop from the weight of heavy emotion, and as Jason surveys the room, everyone else shares a similar expression.

"But enough about my *lovely* past," he says, hoping to ease the tension. "There's something else we need to discuss while we're here."

His team does their best to shake off the anguish that has formed as Jenny responds, "What's that, Coach?"

"Well, I received a three-game suspension for my actions, and they won't even let me onto the practice field until the suspension is over."

"Woo, vacation!" Taya pipes in.

Jason tilts his head in her direction and raises his eyebrows.

"Sorry, just trying to lighten the mood," she replies, throwing her hands up in feigned outrage.

Jason chuckles. "So, for the next eleven days, I'll need—"

"Coach," Sam interjects, "don't worry. We got this. You can serve your suspension, and we'll hold down the fort while you're away."

Jason looks at Sam and thinks back to the first day he met her. She insulted him within seconds of their meeting, then stormed out of the room. He never would've guessed that, a little over a month later, he'd be sitting around a table having this conversation with her, but life is funny that way.

"Works for me," he replies, just as they hear a knock at the door.

Taya hollers, "Food's here!" and then leaps out of her chair, sprinting toward the door to get it.

Jason sees Maddy get up from her chair and walk toward the refreshments laid out in the kitchen, so he stands and follows. She's refilling her glass from the punch bowl by the sink as Jason approaches. He reaches for the chrome handle of the faucet to refill his glass from the tap, then turns in her direction.

"So, you and Nicole seem to have worked things out. How'd that go?"

Maddy doesn't move her head. She just stands there in front of the punch bowl as a smile grows on her face.

***

It's late, and Maddy is walking toward her sister's room. There are two days until the Prescott Ridge game, but that's the last thing on her mind. When she arrives at Nicoles room, the door is open, and she sees Nicole sitting at her computer in the corner. Upon noticing Maddy, she gives a curt look in her direction before returning to the screen and continuing her work.

Maddy drops her head in emotional distress before saying, "Nicole . . . can we please talk?"

"About what?" Nicole shoots back. "You want to yell at me some more for trying to better myself?"

"No . . . I just . . . I want to explain."

"Explain what? That you're jealous I want to go do something new with my life?"

"What? I'm not jealous. It's just . . ."

"It's just, what?"

The pain bubbling up inside Maddy is reaching its peak, and as she goes to respond, it all comes pouring out. "I'm afraid we won't talk anymore if you leave! I'm afraid you'll make new friends, and I'll just be a long-lost footnote in your life! I'm afraid . . . I'm afraid . . ." she hesitates, trying to collect herself. "I'm afraid you'll forget about me!"

Maddy is short of breath, and Nicole looks back at her with a blank face. "Maddy . . . that's ridiculous."

"Then w-why . . . why didn't you tell me you wanted to leave?"

"Because . . . I don't know. I just didn't feel like talking about it until it was real. My transfer hasn't even been accepted yet." She pauses. "Wait . . . So, that's why you've been upset? You thought I was abandoning you?"

"Y-yeah," Maddy replies, teary-eyed.

"Maddy, you're my twin sister, and I love you. No amount of distance between us could ever change what we have. Hell, I'm scared about this decision too."

"You are?"

"Yes. I'm scared about moving to a new place, about being alone and having to branch out, without you there to help me . . . It's terrifying. Maddy, I would never forget you. I'll always want you in my life."

***

"I'll always want you in my life."

Nicole's words still make Maddy smile just as big now as they did three days ago when this conversation took place. The smile on her face continues to grow as she fills her glass from the punch bowl in front of her.

"Maddy? Did you hear me?" Jason's voice snaps her out of the trance. "How'd it go with Nicole?"

She turns in his direction and takes a sip of the punch. "Very good, Coach. Very good."

CHAPTER 21

"Woo! Here we go, ladies!"

Jason is seated on a corner barstool inside The Iron Penn, with an ice-cold old-fashioned resting on the bar in front of him, gracefully set atop a charcoal-colored slate coaster. He is ten days into his eleven-day suspension, and his eyes are permanently fixed on the TV screen mounted above the bar. Jason was radiating with joy after his team had managed to pull out a win in both of their first two games of his suspension, and now, he is impatiently watching them warm up as their third game is about to begin.

"How are you feeling, Jason?" Lucy asks from behind the bar. "Nervous?"

"Well, if we win today, it means we'll clinch a playoff spot for the first time in five years. So, yeah . . . a little nervous."

"I'm sure they're going to do great!" she adds with a smile. "But why are you watching it here? Why not watch from the stands?"

Hmm . . . good question, he thinks. Jason had watched the last two games from his apartment, trying his best to remain hidden from the noise that had been circulating about his *incident.* Some people were extremely supportive, saying things like, "That guy had it coming," and "I would've done the same thing." However, there were others who were nowhere near as kind and understanding. "You should be ashamed of yourself!" "Fire him!" "What kind of example are you setting?" These were just a few of the things he'd heard from outraged people.

While Jason didn't feel that ashamed about his actions, he was admittedly surprised he hadn't been fired. He borderline assaulted a man, and a three-game suspension seemed like a slap on the wrist compared to what could've happened. But as for today's game, he felt the need to get out of his apartment, and he figured Lucy of all people would offer some support.

"Honestly, Lucy, I don't think the people in those stands want to be anywhere near me. They either hate me, or they're afraid of me."

"Well, Jason, I don't hate you, and I'm not afraid of you either. So stay as long as you like," she says with a wink.

There's that playful flirtation, he thinks, still unsure if she's just being polite, or maybe it's something more.

"Thank you."

While Jason grabs his cocktail and takes a sip, he thanks the heavens that today's game got moved from this morning to a night game. Typically, having to wait all day for the game to happen would lead to unwanted anxiety, but with the stress of playoffs looming, and his suspension coming to an end, he's happy it's late enough in the day for him to justify the old-fashioned.

"Woo!" he screams out again, watching Daisy beat her defender and effortlessly place the ball in the back of the net.

"Hey! There we go!" Lucy cheers, clapping as she watches along with him.

While they are resetting play after the goal, she turns to Jason. "Don't you want to be there if they win?"

"Of course, I'd love to be there. But I'd want to be by their side, and they won't let me on the field, or even in the field house."

"Right . . . But once this game ends, doesn't that effectively end your suspension?"

"I mean . . . I guess *technically* you're right . . . But I don't want to rock the boat. I'll just wait until tomorrow."

"Okay . . ."

"What?" Jason asks.

"I'm just saying, if I were them, and I had a new coach come in and do what you've done . . . I'd want you by my side if we won, that's all."

And with that, Lucy goes to serve another customer at the far end of the bar. *Maybe she's right,* he thinks, finishing the last sip of his cocktail.

"You know what, Lucy . . . I think you're right. Why don't you close me out. I've got a team to go support."

"Sure thing. And Jason, I'm always right."

***

Jason decides to walk the few blocks it takes to get to campus. With the playoffs hovering in the balance, his body is fraught with restlessness, and the cool breeze is comforting as it brushes over his body, leaving goosebumps all up and down his forearms. The ten-minute walk is just as aesthetically pleasing as it is calming. The lush greenery that lines the cement sidewalk contrasts beautifully with the sapphire-blue sky. As the wind rustles the leaves of the trees, he can hear birds chirping from the branches within. Even as he approaches campus, the beauty simply doesn't stop. Large stone lions stand guard on either side of the towering steel gate that leads into the university grounds.

When he gets closer to the field, he walks by a babbling fountain and runs his fingers through the rippling water. It's cold to the touch but blissfully refreshing as it touches his skin. Jason arrived here only about a month and a half ago, but as he looks around at the sheer beauty of this place, he feels a sense of home. When he thinks back to how terrified he was of moving to a place he'd never been to before, and taking on a new challenge he'd never attempted, he laughs quietly to himself. It seems so silly now. *What was I so afraid of?*

Fweeeeeet!

Jason can hear the whistle coming from the field in the distance. It's a longer whistle, which makes him think someone must've just scored a goal. Seconds later, his thoughts are confirmed.

"Crystal Summit's goal scored by number 15, Taya Johnson!" the announcer hollers over the loudspeaker, his baritone voice buzzing with excitement.

Jason happily shouts, "Hell yeah!" as he presses on toward the field, picking up his pace in excitement.

When Jason gets to the field, he instinctively grabs the hood of his sweatshirt and lifts it up over his head. Although he's not ashamed of what took place less than two weeks ago, he also doesn't really feel the need to explain himself to anyone else. The team knows, and that's all that matters to him. He finds a spot along the fence line, away from the stands, which are filled at about half capacity with the supportive fans of both teams. While Jason looks over the crowd, it still shocks him that a women's lacrosse game doesn't pack the stadium. Lacrosse has often been referred to as "the fastest sport on two feet," and when it's played at the highest level, among teams with true talent, it's almost poetic to watch.

Jason's eyes shift from the stands to the scoreboard. He's ecstatic to see that his girls are up by five goals at the end of the third quarter.

Presently, both teams are on the sidelines as they await the start of the fourth. The team they're facing is Johnson & Bellevue University, and they are currently huddled tightly around their coach, who appears to be drawing up something on a portable whiteboard. She wears an expression of pure determination that Jason appreciates—even though she's the opposition, it always brings him comfort when he sees a coach that cares.

Across from them, Jason's squad is all huddled together, and it looks like Sam has taken the lead in addressing the team. He's fairly far away, so Jason can't hear what she's saying, but judging by her body language, it seems to him like she's doing a fine job keeping everyone focused and motivated. *Do these girls even need me?* he thinks with a small grin, and he contemplates the fact that a win today would mean a four-game winning streak that he wasn't even a part of.

The horn sounds, signifying the fourth quarter is about to begin, and Jason lets out a deep exhale as he prepares to watch the final quarter unfold.

Within the first few minutes, Jason can already tell what the opposing team had been discussing between quarters. Both Maddy and Nicole are being aggressively faceguarded by their defenders, completely blanketed and unable to touch the ball. Faceguarding has always been a simple, yet effective plan—the idea being that if the other team has players who are exceptionally talented, if you don't let them touch the ball, they can't score—which is clearly the plan Johnson & Bellevue's coach has put into motion. The only problem with this plan is that it allows other players on the field more space than they'd usually have, so one-on-one dodges are typically the best way to disrupt this strategy. As Jason watches on in suspense, he wishes more and more that he could be on the sideline with his team—not just because he wants to coach them on this strategy, but because he's also genuinely missing being around them. He still remembers what Chuck had told him back when he first arrived on campus and was struggling to connect with the team.

"There are other ways to relate to people; there are other ways to open up."

He was certainly right about that. Jason had never opened up about his past to anyone else like he had with the team, and he felt remarkably closer to them after he did.

Twelve minutes later, Jason can feel himself becoming increasingly on edge as the seconds tick away. With three minutes remaining in the game, Maddy and Nicole are still completely locked off and unable to contribute. The five-goal lead they entered the fourth quarter with has dwindled down to one, with a current score of 18–17, and the opposing team's offense is showing no signs of slowing down.

"Come on, girls, you got this," he says nervously. "Just get one more goal for insurance and then hold on to that lead and kill the clock to victory."

With two minutes now remaining, the opposition is barreling towards the Blue Jays' goal with ferocity, and Jason holds his breath. If they score and tie the game up, with such a short amount of time remaining, that momentum will surely give them a huge advantage if the game goes into overtime. Jason can barely stand to watch, and he continues nervously speaking to himself in an effort to stay calm.

"Come on, girls, this is no time for caution. Play aggressively and go get the ball."

A chill runs down his spine when he sees Rachel leap to intercept a pass.

Did she fucking hear me?

Time appears to slow as she pushes off her back foot and flies through the air toward the ball. Jason looks on with anticipation, trying not to blink for fear of missing it. When she lands, the ball ends up firmly inside her stick, and she takes off sprinting, full steam ahead in the other direction.

"Woo!" Jason screams with excitement, and a few fans who are nearby turn in his direction.

He lifts his hand to cover his face, attempting to hide his identity. To Jason's relief, the fans turn away, and he turns his attention back to the game.

Rachel is cruising down the field at an exceptional pace, with every stride carrying her farther and faster toward the goal. As she crosses the thirty-yard restraining line, the defenders who are faceguarding the twins stay locked onto Maddy and Nicole, and Rachel sees her opening. She takes a few steps forward before changing direction and running parallel to the net. Jason can see her arms cock back to wind up while she runs, planting her feet with every step—*left foot, right foot, left foot.*

"Deep breath, Rachel," Jason whispers. "Don't overthink it."

She takes one final step, then lets the ball fly. Jason finds himself once again holding his breath in anticipation as the entire stadium goes silent.

Dink!

The sound echoes throughout the field as the ball hits the inside of the post and ricochets into the net behind the goalie. For a second, no one moves at all. Then suddenly, there's an eruption. Fans in the stands boom with excitement, and a slow, steady chant can be heard emanating from all around the field.

"Rachel."

"Rachel!"

"Rachel!"

The chant builds, getting even louder and more intense as more people join in.

"Rachel!"

"RACHEL!"

"RAACHEL!"

As the chanting reverberates throughout the stadium, goosebumps return to Jason's arms, and an ear-to-ear smile grows across his face. Elation doesn't even begin to describe the emotion coursing through him when, moments later, the final whistle sounds, and he gets to watch his team storm the field in celebration.

Jason waits impatiently until they eventually calm down and line up to shake the opposing team's hands. Although he's too far away to hear, he can see them all mouthing the words, "Good game," as they pass by one another. Jason is bouncing his right leg rapidly, waiting for the lines to finish. Once the final players shake hands, he can't help himself as he jumps the fence and storms the field toward them. Chloe is the first to see him coming.

"Coach!" she announces loudly.

"You made it!" Rachel says.

"I wouldn't miss this for the world!" Jason replies. "Ladies . . . we're going to the playoffs!"

This announcement sends a shockwave throughout the team as they jump up and down with excitement. During the celebration, Jason realizes this might be the happiest he's felt in a long time. He has a new family, and as he watches them revel in their victory, a strong feeling of fulfillment flows throughout his body.

After a few more minutes of celebrating, Sam looks at Jason. "So, Coach, anything you want to say before we head inside?"

"Yes, there is, Sam . . . I am so proud of you." Jason can already feel he's getting a bit choked up. "You all did something today that no one expected. Whether or not my actions during the Prescott Ridge game were justified, there's no denying it set us back. But you didn't let that bring you down; instead, you let it fuel you. You rallied in the face of adversity, and you came out the other side stronger, better people. So remember this feeling, and take it with you when times get tough, as a reminder that nothing will ever be able to stop you, so long as you believe in yourself."

"Well fucking said," Sam replies.

"Want to break us down, Captain?"

"Eh, I think this one's all you, Coach."

Jason lifts his hand to the sky. "Sticks up!" he yells, and the team follows suit. "Jays on three—one, two, three, Jays!"

As the team heads into the locker room, Jason takes a seat on the sideline bench and leans his head back, looking upward at the tranquil blue sky. The field has nearly cleared out, and it's become eerily quiet in the twenty minutes or so since the final whistle sounded. Jason sits there, listening, as the stillness around him brings a semblance of calm after the culmination of the thrilling game that just transpired. The birds are still chirping softly as they fly through the air. He can hear the distinct *crunch* of tires rolling on pavement as the last of the cars pull out of the parking lot. Then he hears a sound that stands out amongst the rest—a small, seemingly insignificant sound that penetrates his eardrum.

Clang . . . clang . . . clang!

The American flag waves in the wind, and the rope starts to make the all too familiar noise, which causes Jason's arm to tremble. The noise persists and grows in intensity.

Clang . . . clang . . . clang!

Clang . . . clang! CLANG!

CLANG! CLANG! CLANG!

Jason's vision goes white, and his head becomes faint. *What the fuck? No. No. This can't be happening again.* His mind is racing as his ears begin to ring. A strong feeling of hopelessness washes over him as nausea kicks in, and he feels like he may pass out. *Why? Why is this happening?* His brain tries to fight back. He closes his eyes and clenches his fists as he begins to hyperventilate. Without warning, tears flow from his eyes like a faucet as his body starts to shake. Just as he feels his body giving in, he hears it: the sound of cleats on turf.

At first, the sound is faint, but it gets louder as the footsteps approach. Jason is still very much in a state of shock, and he's afraid to open his eyes. As the footsteps pass by him, they stop, and someone sits down next to him. He waits, still shaking and doing his best to control the terror that is desperately trying to escape him. As he waits in anticipation, time seems to drag on forever until the person next to him finally speaks.

"Hey, Coach . . . You look like shit, you know that?"

Jason spits out a laugh, interrupting his sobs. Sam's comment does exactly what she intended, disarming the tension with a dash of humor and sincerity. Her words of endearment lift his spirits ever so slightly as his body stops shaking, little by little. He still feels weak, but after a few seconds pass, his ears stop ringing . . . He opens his eyes . . . He's not alone.

PART III

THE LEAP

CHAPTER 22

"Sam, thank you for coming back out."

"Well, Coach, I actually came out to grab my stick that I'd forgotten, but then I saw you sitting here crying. And you know, when I see a wounded puppy, I always get the urge to help."

Her words of endearment continue to lift his spirits, as she no longer uses the harsh, malicious tone he's grown accustomed to.

"Well, I appreciate it, I really do."

They sit there on the bench for a while, not feeling the need to say anything, just enjoying each other's presence.

A few minutes pass, and Sam decides to break the silence. "I used to have a brother."

Jason whips his head in her direction. "What?"

"I had a brother. His name was John, and he also died when I was young."

"Sam . . . are you serious?"

"Yeah. He had a rare blood disorder. We found out early on, so we knew our time with him was limited, and I cherished every second we shared together. But even after months of knowing it was coming, when he passed . . . It fucking hurt. It still fucking hurts. Every day."

"Fuck . . . Sam, I don't know what to say. I'm so sorry." Jason's own emotions are bubbling back up as she remains stone-faced, looking forward.

"After he passed, everyone just wanted to help. Every teacher I had, every relative, every friend, every coach . . . They all thought they had the solution to solve my sadness. But the truth is, the only solution would've been to have my brother back. And they couldn't give me that. So, every time they tried to help, it just made me angry."

"Jesus . . . No wonder you didn't like me when I came here." In an attempt to lighten the conversation, Jason lets out a small chuckle, but when Sam turns her head, her eyes are filled with sadness.

"Coach . . . I'm so sorry. All you've done since you arrived was try to help us, and I was a fucking bitch to you every step along the way."

"Sam, it's okay."

"No, it's not, though. I mean"—she sniffles—"some of the things I said were so out of line . . . You should be pissed at me."

"It's like you said, loss is hard. We try to handle it as best we can, but there's no user manual for what we've been through. So, sometimes, we still come up short. I mean, for God's sake, I've had over a decade to process my sister's death, and as you can see, I'm still pretty fucking far from okay."

"I guess you're right . . . But I still feel bad."

"We should've talked about this weeks ago," Jason says. "It feels good to talk about it."

"Communication is the key."

The words effortlessly fall from Sam's mouth, and Jason turns to her and tilts his head. "Communication is the key?"

"Yeah, sorry, that's an old mantra my therapist used to tell me. She says talking things out will always help you release the burden of pain that may be holding you down."

"Shit, that's deep, and insightful. Any other words of wisdom she's told you that might help me out?"

"Yeah, she always says—" Sam stops short. "Wait, Coach, have you never been to therapy?"

Jason looks to the ground and shakes his head softly. "I have not."

"You should . . . Sorry, I don't know if I'm crossing a line by saying that."

Jason lifts his head and lets out a chuckle.

"Coach?"

"Sorry, it's just, you're not the first person to utter those words. My mentor would love to know you just said that."

"Is this the same mentor that helped you after Syracuse?"

"Yup. His name is Chuck. Honestly, without him, my life might've taken a much darker path. He tells me constantly I should try therapy."

"If you don't mind my asking . . . Why haven't you?"

"Because I'm afraid," Jason blurts out without thinking.

"Coach, respectfully, what are you so afraid of?"

That's a fair question, he thinks. Jason had spent the last few months telling every player on this team that, as long as they try, they'll never fail. Yet, for some reason, he was too afraid to try.

"I'm not quite sure. I think the idea of being that vulnerable . . . it just scares me."

"I get that, I do . . . but, Coach, how's it feel talking to me right now about this?"

"It feels great."

"And how did it feel when you told the team about your sister?"

"Also great," he replies, then lets out a laugh. "Fuuuck . . . You're right. I'd been holding on to those feelings for a while. It felt so good to get them off my chest."

"That's therapy, Coach," she replies with a shrug. "Well, that's not all therapy is, but it's some of it. Talking things out, releasing burdens; it's cathartic."

Jason takes this all in as he looks off into the distance. Chuck has told him for years he should try therapy, but this might be the first time he's actually considering it.

"You might be right, Sam . . . Maybe I'll try it."

"I know it's scary, but I promise it's worth it."

"So, what was the other piece of wisdom you were going to tell me?" Jason asks.

"Huh?"

"Before you asked if I had ever been to therapy, you were about to tell me something your therapist always likes to say."

"Oh, right," Sam replies. "She always tells me, 'Your past doesn't dictate your future.'"

Jason leans back.

"Damn, I like that . . . Maybe I should take the leap."

"Take the leap," Sam says. "Well, I like that."

They both just sit there for a while, neither one wanting to leave. While enjoying each other's company and relishing the new bond they've formed, Jason's shoulders finally relax a bit, possibly for the first time in weeks. With every breath he takes, it's as if a weight is lifted off his chest. As he looks at Sam, he's reminded of everything that's happened over the last few months between them. How she immediately rejected his authority on the first day they met. How she had said so many awful things to express her distaste toward him. How she insulted him every chance she got, reminding him constantly that she didn't respect him as a coach.

Looking at her now, all he can do is smile, thinking about how far they've come. He knew from very early on that if this team was going to succeed, Sam was the domino that needed to fall. But since then, it's become far more than that. There's a kinship between them, a kinship formed through shared trauma and honest communication. A kinship that grows stronger with every second they sit together on this cold, metal bench.

"Well, you ready to go?"

"I am, Coach," she replies, then adds, "Three more games until the playoffs. We've got work to do."

Now with a newfound purpose in their eyes, they both stand and make their way off the field. Every step brings Jason hope— a hope that he hasn't felt in a long, long time.

CHAPTER 23

As Jason sits in his office, feeling proud of what he and his team have accomplished, his attention drifts to the whiteboard attached to the wall. The board is filled with the current standings of every team within their conference. As he looks toward the glossy, marked-up surface, he is still in awe at what he sees.

Playoff Teams:

1. *Emerald Hills University – (Clinched Bye Week)*

2. *Crystal Summit University – (Clinched Bye Week)*

3. *Prescott Ridge University*

4. *Johnson & Bellevue University*

5. *Sunnyview Hollows University*

6. *Holstead Valley University*

Eliminated Teams:

7. *James Williamson University*

8. *South Central University*

9. *Northern Peaks University*

10. *Glendale Hills University*

Through the last three games, they secured dominant wins over their opponents, putting them firmly in second place with a conference record of 8–1, with their only loss being to Emerald Hills who is sitting above them in first place.

Vrrr, vrrr. Jason's phone begins to vibrate on his desk. Jason is happy to see from the caller ID that it's his mentor, Chuck, calling him.

"Hey, Chuck!"

"Jason! You're about to go on a playoff run . . . *and* you get a bye week!" Chuck replies, full of excitement as if he were in the room, staring at the same whiteboard Jason is. "How's it feel, bud?"

"Honestly, I'm still shocked. It's just so surreal. If you had told me when I got here that the regular season would end like this . . . I would've thought you were high."

"Ha! Oh, please . . . I never doubted you for a second!"

Jason smiles, knowing full well that he means it. Even if the odds were hopelessly stacked against him, Chuck would still bet on Jason. The thought of his mentor's unwavering belief in him is usually terrifying, but right now, it feels great.

"Well, I appreciate that, Chuck."

"So, I have to ask, aside from the success, how have you been doing since . . . *the incident?*"

Jason hadn't spoken with Chuck much since the Prescott Ridge debacle, and he knew this conversation was coming, but for some reason, he felt oddly comfortable discussing it.

"I'm doing well; it's been pretty busy since then, so I haven't really thought too much about it."

"Has anything happened since then that you want to talk about?"

"I mean . . . not really. Things have been good."

"You do sound different."

"What do you mean?"

"Something about your voice; you sound more . . . confident. More sure of yourself. It's not a bad thing, just an observation."

"I've gotten a lot closer to the team," Jason replies. "After Prescott Ridge, I told them about Lilly."

"Wait, really?"

"Yeah, and I actually had a really nice moment with Sam a few weeks back as well, after our win that clinched us a spot in the playoffs. Apparently, she had a brother that passed away when she was younger, so we connected through that."

"So . . . what you're saying is . . . you opened up to your team, and it felt good?" Chuck replies with a heavy dose of sarcasm.

Jason lets out a deep sigh and chuckles. "Yes, Chuck, you were right all along."

"I always am, Jason. I always am."

"She actually—" Jason stops mid-sentence.

"What is it, Jason?"

He hesitates briefly before deciding to continue. "She told me I should try therapy."

"Well, well, well . . ." Chuck replies. "And? Are you finally considering it?"

"I don't know . . . Maybe. It has felt really good to talk about it. But I also feel kind of bad because you've been telling me to do this for years."

"Jason, it's okay. I never wanted to push you into something you didn't want to do. I'm just glad you're finally considering it. It shows real growth."

Jason doesn't reply. His mind wanders.

"Jason, are you still there?"

"Yeah, sorry. I was just thinking about how much this job has changed me. I mean, imagine if you'd never told me to try coaching so many years ago. Imagine if I'd been too afraid to take this job when it was offered to me. Imagine if I'd given up when things got tough—"

"Jason, stop," Chuck interjects. "You can keep thinking in circles, wondering how you got here, or . . . you can just be happy you're here. Enjoy these small moments of clarity, and remember, everything happens for a reason."

"Ah, you're right, Chuck. You're always right."

"So, what are your plans for the bye week?" Chuck asks, changing the subject.

"I was thinking about setting up a team-bonding event to try and build on the momentum we've made. Do you think that's a good idea?"

"I think that's a *great* idea." Chuck replies, and Jason hears a muffled sniffle through the phone.

"Chuck? You okay?"

"Yes . . . It's just . . . you've come a long way, and I'm really proud of you, Jason."

With this declaration of pride, Jason immediately feels overcome with emotion. He is used to Chuck being motivational and fatherlike, but he's not used to seeing this vulnerable side.

"Thank you, Chuck." Jason barely gets out the words before his lips start to quiver and his eyes well up. "I have to go. I have a . . . a . . . meeting to get to," Jason lies.

"Okay," Chuck replies, and Jason is sure he can tell he's lying. "Well, good luck with the team bonding. Talk soon."

And with that, Chuck hangs up the phone, leaving Jason sitting alone in his office. His body is flooded with happiness and contentment as he pulls the lever on his ergonomic chair, and it gently lowers him toward the ground, letting out a long *whoosh* noise as it sinks. Jason looks to the ceiling and smiles as a tear of joy runs blissfully down his cheek.

CHAPTER 24

"You're going with the 8-pounder?" Jason asks, looking over to Rachel as she lifts a bright orange bowling ball off the rack.

"Yeah, I feel like I can throw the lighter balls faster. Why? Which weight are you choosing?"

Jason reaches for a dark green ball on the top of the rack and raises it up, admiring it. "14-pounder, for sure. I've always found that using a heavier ball, but throwing it with subtlety and composure, is the best way to play."

"But, Coach, nothing you do is subtle or composed," she says with a laugh.

"You may have a point," he replies, and they both walk back toward the rest of their team.

For their bye week, Jason chose bowling for their team-bonding event. It's a fairly active sport, and it gets people oddly competitive. Plus, there's something about hurling a heavy spherical mass down a sixty-foot lane, trying to knock down ten innocent pins, that is just so unbelievably satisfying.

When Jason and Rachel reach the team, they are sitting in booths by their bowling lanes, entering their names into the tiny computer screen affixed to the front of the ball return. They separated themselves into four teams: *The Brick Wall, The Soldiers, The Arsenal,* and—since there were a few extra players—a fourth team made up of Jenny, Sam, Chloe, and Jason. They called their team, *The Champs.*

"The Captains, the Coach, and the Keeper," Sam announces as she enters their names and then turns around to face the rest of the team. "You guys are fucked."

"Ooooo, we're so scared," Nicole taunts from the booth.

"Yeah, look, I'm shaking," Maddy says while raising her arm in the air and shaking it in an exaggerated manner. Sam furrows her brow, and her nostrils flare.

This reaction just makes the twins laugh even harder. Sam whips around and sits down next to Jason.

"Coach, you're up to start," Sam says aloud, before whispering in his ear, "Please tell me you're good at this."

Jason smiles and stands. He approaches the ball return and grabs the dark green sphere, again lifting it up to his face to admire it, then shooting a sidelong glance at Sam with a smirk on his face. She lifts an eyebrow in confusion as Jason turns, takes four steps forward, and launches the ball down the lane. The ball kisses the floor—barely making a sound—then begins to rotate at great speed before smashing into the unsuspecting pins and sending them all flying.

"What was it you two were saying?" Sam mocks as she turns her attention back to Maddy and Nicole.

"Shit," Maddy mutters under her breath.

Jason heads back to the booth and sits down next to Sam.

"So, Coach . . . have you ever bowled before?"

"Three times a month from age ten to age eighteen," he answers. "I guess it is just like riding a bike."

"I guess so."

***

Thirty minutes later, the competitive nature of the team-bonding event is still in full swing. *The Brick Wall* team is far ahead of *The Soldiers* and *The Arsenal,* but *The Champs* are sitting handily in first place as Jenny gets up to bowl.

Chloe hollers, "You got this, Jenny!" as Jenny walks toward the lane, holding her bright pink 10-pound ball in position, ready to launch it toward the pins.

She takes a few steps, then releases the ball. It starts off straight, but quickly veers off and misses the front pin, causing only seven pins to fall. Two pins stand off to the right, and the center pin stands separate and alone.

"You know the goal is to knock them all down at once, right?" Taya teases from the next lane over.

Jenny doesn't register the insult. She keeps her eyes pointed down the lane, debating her next shot.

"I think I'm going to go for the two pins on the right. Nine is a solid frame," she announces. "We'll still be able to win if I only get nine."

"I think if you go for that front pin and hit it at the right angle, you can knock it into the others and pick up the spare," Jason counters.

Jenny looks back down the lane. "I don't know; it seems risky . . . I could hit the front pin at the wrong angle, or I could miss it completely. The safe bet is to go for the two pins together."

"Okay, your call," Jason replies as she lifts her ball back into position and prepares to throw.

It isn't long after her release that it becomes obvious the ball will not hit its mark. It rolls off course about halfway down the lane and sails into the gutter, missing the two pins completely.

"Damnit!" Jenny says, pouting as she storms back to the booth.

"Ha! Jenny, you're supposed to keep the ball between those two gutters, not in them!" Maddy jeers.

Jesus, these girls are ruthlessly competitive, Jason thinks, and Jenny plops back down into the booth with a huff. He can see the competitive nature in her eyes as she stares straight ahead, clearly frustrated. This is just a simple game, but she's taking it seriously. *That must be what makes her such a good captain.*

To distract her and to help better her mood, Jason decides to change topics. "So, Jenny, any more news on that space for lease you were looking into?"

"What?" she responds, her mind still clearly focused on the last frame.

"The lease for the bagel place you're thinking of opening. The one we talked about at our mid-season meeting."

"Oh . . . right. I did think more about it, but I don't know if I'm going to do it."

"Wait, why?"

"I . . . I just don't think it's the right move for me right now, you know?"

"No . . . I don't know. You said you've been thinking about this bagel shop for nearly fourteen years."

"I know, it's just . . . It's a huge risk. The safe bet would be for me to go work in the business industry and get a job in accounting or banking. Then maybe a few years down the road, when I've saved up some money, I could try my bagel shop idea."

"Jenny, if that's what you truly think is best for you, then I'll drop it. But . . ."

"But what?"

"I just hate seeing people waste their potential," Jason replies flatly, "and I'm not saying that you wouldn't make a fine accountant or banker. I just think if you have a dream, now's the time to chase it, that's all."

"I know . . . but the safe bet—"

"Jenny, stop for a second," Jason interjects. "Do you want me to be a supportive friend right now, or an honest coach?"

"I always want you to be honest; there's no need to sugarcoat it for me, Coach."

"Okay, great. Then enough with this *safe bet* nonsense."

"What?"

"Jenny, I know it can be scary, but even if you take the safe bet, you can still fail. I mean, take those pins, for example." Jason gestures toward the bowling lane. "You went for the safe bet, and you still ended up missing."

"I don't know if I'm following you, Coach."

"All I'm saying is, whether you take the risky approach or you play it safe, you can still come up short. So, if failure is always a possibility, why not chase your dreams?"

"I know you're right . . . But where would I even start?"

"Step one is easy: You have to call that landlord and discuss the space they're leasing."

"Geez, pretty big step one, don't you think?"

"I know, Jenny, but the truth is, the first step is always the biggest. It's acknowledging to yourself that you're ready to do this. That you're ready to go all in. That you're ready to take the leap."

Jenny nods her head in thought. "Thanks, Coach. I think I needed this talk."

"Anytime, Jenny, anytime," he says with a smile. "Now, let me ask you this . . . How are you feeling about the playoffs?"

"We're going to dominate."

"I like your confidence, but it's a long road ahead."

"Coach, mark my words, in a few short weeks, when you're staring at the full playoff bracket, you'll see our name in the championship slot," Jenny replies, her confidence even more prevalent than before.

"Well, alright, then."

"Hey, Jenny, you're up!" Chloe announces as the pins reset themselves at the end of the lane.

Jenny stands to take her turn. While Jason watches her walk to the ball return and pick up the bright pink sphere, he thinks about what she said and imagines hoisting the championship trophy above his head. The entire team stands around him, screaming so loud in excitement that he can't even hear himself think, but he doesn't care. Because at that moment, everything is right with the world.

"We got this," he says under his breath. "We got this."

CHAPTER 25

It's 9:30 a.m. on the morning of their semi-final game. Jason sits alone on a cold aluminum chair in the center of the locker room. The air is dry and still. The fluorescent light above him has been flickering every few minutes since he arrived nearly four hours ago, unable to sleep in anticipation of today's game. His eyes are haunted by the board in front of him. On the board sits the current playoff bracket. During the bye week, Sunnyview Hollows managed to upset Johnson & Bellevue, so they will play at Emerald Hills today in a game that will surely end in their defeat. On the other side of the bracket sits today's matchup for Jason and his Crystal Summit Blue Jays. Prescott Ridge took down Holstead Valley, so they will be making the trip back up to Crystal Summit today.

Though his incident with one of their fans happened over a month ago, he's certain they haven't forgotten, and it's leaving him with an uneasy feeling sitting heavy in the pit of his stomach. Jason always knew this was a possibility. Prescott Ridge was the clear favorite in their first-round matchup, but he'd been holding out hope that they'd somehow lose, and spare him the trouble of coaching in front of that crowd again. But alas, luck isn't on his side. While his eyes remain hooked on the board, voices coming from outside the door release him from his trance. The team has arrived.

Sam is the first to enter the room, and Jason's presence catches her off guard.

"Fuck!" she yells out, startled. "What the hell are you doing here so early, Coach?"

Jason shrugs. "Couldn't sleep. I felt antsy, so I came here," he replies, feeling no reason to lie, as the rest of the team enters and takes a seat at their lockers.

"Shit. Well, okay, then, but wait . . . where's your suit?"

Jason almost forgot he chose not to come dressed in a suit today—though he did bring one with him to the field house. It's a special suit he'd been saving for their first playoff game. The suit is a vibrant shade of powder blue, and he also has a matching powder blue tie, a tie clip, a lapel pin, and a pocket silk. The suit is definitely a statement piece, but Jason has been postponing wearing it.

"It's hanging in that bag over there." Jason gestures toward a large black bag hanging in a vacant corner locker. "But . . . I'm not sure if I'm going to wear it."

"What? But why, Coach?" Jenny replies.

"Ladies, there's no reason to sugarcoat it; this Prescott Ridge crowd is going to be a fucking nightmare today, and I don't know if my adding fuel to the fire by wearing a bright blue suit is the right thing to do . . . It's just—"

"Fuck that," Rachel interjects.

Jason recoils as he looks toward her. He can't say for sure, but he's pretty sure this is the first time he's ever heard her swear.

"Excuse me?"

"I said. Fuck. That," she replies, doubling down. "Coach, you have spent the last few months teaching us to never give up and to believe in ourselves. Don't let these vicious pricks stop you from being who you are."

Jason's eyebrows raise in astonishment. "Damn. Well, alright, then. I think I like this side of you, Rachel. The truth is, ladies, this is going to be a game unlike any we've played thus far. The crowd will probably be on us from the instant we step onto the field. The players won't have forgotten about my outburst either, and they will most likely try to provoke us—do not let them. We play our game, and we fucking win."

"Well said, Coach. Any specific notes for defense? They definitely hammered us pretty hard last game," Sam asks.

"Y-yeah, they r-really took a lot of shots on me last game . . ." Chloe stammers, visibly nervous.

"You're going to do great, Chloe," Luna says, and Chloe looks up at her, beginning to blush.

"Thanks," she replies, then quickly looks away.

"Yes, Sam, my notes for defense are simple," Jason takes back over, "They like to play fast, and they'll be expecting us to play it safe. So let's catch them off guard. Be aggressive, press out, and disrupt."

"Oo-Fuckin'-Ra, Commander."

"Oo-Fuckin'-Ra, indeed," Jason replies. "I'll give you all a few minutes to get dressed, then meet me in the hallway, and we can head out onto the field and show these Grizzlys that this is our fucking house."

The team explodes in a frenzy of animalistic cheers. Jason grabs his suit, then gives Chloe a quick glance and gestures for her to come over. She tilts her head in a puzzled manner, but gets up and follows him out of the locker room.

"Hey . . . What's up, Coach?"

"I just wanted to make sure you're doing okay. You seemed a little nervous in there, so I wanted to check in."

"I am a little shaky."

"Hey, this is a big game. Pregame jitters are completely normal," Jason assures her.

"I know, it's just . . ." Chloe glances toward the locker room door apprehensively.

"You still haven't talked to Luna, have you?"

Chloe looks away shyly before shaking her head.

"Chloe, can I ask you something?"

She looks at him, still appearing a bit timid to talk.

"I don't want to press, and if you don't want to talk about this, or if I'm just way off base, let me know . . . But does your hesitation to talk with Luna have anything to do with your mother?"

"What? Why would you say that?"

"Well . . . I overheard a conversation before our Emerald Hills matchup about how she wasn't coming to a game—"

Jason stops when he sees that Chloe's eyes are welling up with tears.

"Oh, my God, Chloe . . . I'm so sorry. I shouldn't have pried."

"No, it's okay . . ." Chloe sniffles. "You're not wrong." She exhales deeply to compose herself before continuing. "When I came out to my parents, I was on the verge of all-out tears, not knowing how they would react. But my dad was immediately accepting of me. He gave me a big hug and then asked me so many thoughtful questions, wanting to make sure I felt comfortable. It was such a great feeling, but then I looked over at my mom and saw that her face was pale and blank. She just shook her head and walked away . . ." Chloe stops again, now on the verge of tears. "It was the saddest day of my life . . . She was ashamed of me."

"Chloe, thank you for sharing that with me, but can I ask . . . Why doesn't she come to our lacrosse games?"

"Well, I only told my parents this about eight months ago, before I came to college, so I haven't really spoken to her much since then . . . I guess she just doesn't want to see me . . ." More tears fall from her eyes, and she wipes them away. "I really want to tell Luna how I feel. I'm honestly not even really nervous about what she'll say. It's just . . ."

"You're holding back because of your mom," Jason says— assuming her thought—and Chloe nods in agreement.

"I just don't want to give her any reason to hate me . . ."

"Chloe, I feel I should say again that I am definitely unqualified to give advice on this situation . . . But I do know what it's like to love someone, to care about someone unconditionally. So, believe me when I say, she doesn't hate you. I'm sure she cares about you and loves you deeply. She probably just needs some time . . . But, Chloe, just because she may need time, doesn't mean you should waste yours."

"What do you mean?"

"You just heard Rachel tell me that I shouldn't let those . . . Oh, what were the words she used to delicately describe the Prescott Ridge fans? . . . Oh, right, 'vicious pricks.' She said I shouldn't let those vicious pricks stop me from being who I am. Now, I'm not calling your mom a prick—"

Chloe chuckles, then gives Jason a warm smile. Jason laughs with her.

"But Rachel's message remains true. Don't let the opinions of others stop you from being who you are. If you want something, go out there and get it. You've gotta take the leap."

"Thank you, Coach. I really appreciate it."

"My pleasure. Why don't you take a little time in the locker room to get ready? We'll meet you out there, okay?"

"Sounds good."

Jason heads into the bathroom adjacent to the locker room to get dressed up in his suit. Before long, he's standing in front of the mirror and examining his look. The slight color difference between the blues that make up his suit and its accessories, combined with the black rims of his sunglasses and lapel, makes it almost look like he's a giant blue jay himself.

"Holy shit!" He laughs. "Yeah . . . This is definitely going to draw some attention."

As he is exiting the bathroom, the locker room door opens.

"Coach! Now that's what I call a goddamn suit," Maddy announces.

"You're a Blue Jay!" Nicole adds.

"That's the idea. Now, who's ready to kick some ass?"

"Let's do this," Jenny chimes in, and they turn to head outside toward the field.

The hallway seems longer than usual as Jason leads the team down it. The lighting always creates a strange tunnel vision effect as he walks, but today, every step makes it appear to stretch even farther as the double doors slowly come into view. Jason is the first to the doors, and as he pushes them open, the sunlight floods in. At first, it seems like any other game day, but as he takes a few more steps out into the light, he hears it.

"*Boooooo!*"

The booing echoes throughout the stadium as Jason emerges into view. He can feel the *boos* deep in his chest. This isn't just a small group of fans—this is hundreds of bitter, outraged people showing their collective contempt for Jason all at once. At first, his body locks up, and his mind races, making it seem like his head is spinning. But before the panic can fully set in, Jason feels a hand on his shoulder. He turns to see Sam right by his side, with a fiery look in her eyes.

"Coach, this is your moment . . . And these bastards don't control you. Make sure they fucking know it."

Jason takes a deep inhale through his nose, then gives a single nod back to Sam before turning toward the crowd. He lifts his arms up to the sky, begging them for more.

"*Boooooo!*" they shout in response.

Jason doubles down and brings one hand up to his ear, gesturing as if to say, "Is that all you got? I can't hear you!"

"*Boooooo!*"

The crowd doesn't relent, but that just makes him smile even wider.

Never stop, he thinks. Sam is right. This is his moment, and he won't let anyone take that away from him.

Eventually, the noise from the crowd dies down, and the teams take the field to warm up. Jason takes a seat on the bench, allowing his legs to rest in the shade while the team stretches.

Luna approaches him and says, "Hey, Coach, I'll be right back. I forgot my mouthguard in the locker room."

"No problem," he replies, and she walks back into the field house.

***

Chloe has been sitting in her locker with her head down for what feels like hours, but she knows it can't have been more than a few minutes. Her nerves have calmed a bit, and she's becoming more and more relaxed as the minutes go by. The goalie stick that lies in front of her has been picked clean of tape over the last week, a telltale sign that she's been stressed. Just as she lets out a deep exhale and raises her head, the door swings open and startles her.

"Oh, hey, sorry! I didn't know anyone was in here," Luna says.

"That's okay," Chloe replies, smiling and turning away just at the sight of her.

Luna walks over to her locker and starts to root around in the clothing that is haphazardly thrown about.

"Forgot my mouthguard," she says, continuing to search.

"Oh, I'm sure it's over there somewhere!" Chloe replies nervously, but she wants to say so much more.

Her breathing speeds up, and she can feel butterflies in her stomach.

"Got it!" Luna announces, raising the mouthguard in the air. "Well, I'll see you out there!"

As Luna walks toward the door, the butterflies in Chloe's stomach are now flapping around like crazy. She goes to call out but hesitates, feeling frozen in time.

Luna is nearly out the door when Chloe finally speaks. "Wait!"

"What's up?" she replies, turning toward Chloe and letting the door close behind her.

"I . . . I have to tell you something."

"Okay, what is it?"

"I . . . I . . ."

She can't seem to get the words out.

"I . . ."

"What is it, Chloe?" Luna can tell she's struggling and moves in closer. "Chloe, you can tell me anythi—"

"I like you," she blurts out.

The words fly from her mouth and float through the air. Luna's face is motionless as she processes the information, and Chloe can't get a read on her. The butterflies that were flapping around in her stomach only seconds before are now swirling around like a tornado, and a feeling of nausea takes over as her breathing becomes more and more rapid.

Luna goes to speak, but Chloe cuts her off. "Sorry. No, I didn't mean that. Obviously, you don't like me back." She places her face in her hands with embarrassment as she continues to spiral. "I'm sorry. I'm sorry . . . I should just go."

Chloe stands to leave, but Luna places her hand on her shoulder, stopping her. "Chloe," she says, looking deep into her eyes.

"Luna, y-you don't have to s-say anything, okay. I . . . I . . . I shouldn't have put you on the spot. I'm just going to go. I'll see you out ther—"

"I like you too."

Chloe freezes, and her eyes grow wide as she stands there with her mouth agape. A smile slowly sprouts across her face as the butterflies in her stomach fly away. Her breathing slows, and her body shakes with joy as euphoria flows through her.

"You do?" Chloe responds, not knowing what else to say, and still very much in shock.

"I do," Luna replies, and all at once they fall into each other's arms and share a warm embrace.

Blissful glee fills her soul, and her cheeks strain from smiling, as she can't remember the last time she felt this free. She put herself out there and came out the other side okay . . . She took the leap.

***

Fweet! Fweet! Fweeeeeeeet!

The final whistle blows as the announcer's voice booms throughout the stadium: "And that's the game, folks! Your Crystal Summit Blue Jays come out victorious with a final score of 13–3, and I've got to say all the credit goes to some outstanding goalkeeping by your very own Chloe Harrington!"

Jason looks out upon his team as they storm the field and give Chloe the celebration she deserves after a performance like that. While they dance around screaming, a thought pops into Jason's head, and he can't control the grin that grows across his face.

Holy shit . . . we're going to the fucking championship.

CHAPTER 26

"Alright, ladies, bring it in!" Jason yells out across the field.

It feels like a fairytale watching his team close in on him, jogging over in their powder blue pinnies, like a band of blue jays circling the nest. It had been a long week of practice after the semifinal win against Prescott Ridge, and Jason hadn't wasted any time getting the team back on the field to prepare for their championship matchup. Now, with the game only twenty-four hours away, the excitement within the team has risen to an all-time high.

"Before we leave for the day, I wanted to take some time to discuss tomorrow's game."

"It had to be Emerald Hills, didn't it?" Taya says aloud, to no one in particular.

"Hey, every compelling story needs a strong ending; it's almost poetic," Jason replies. "But I want to have a quick chat to make sure that we're the ones who end up on top tomorrow."

"Do you still want me to faceguard their strong attacker?" Luna asks. "What was her name . . . Jamie? Julia—"

"Juliana Richards," Jason interjects. "And yes, I do. But there is something you should know."

"What's that?"

"Prior to our last matchup, I was told that Juliana wanted to transfer to our team next year."

The team looks around at each other with raised eyebrows.

"Coach . . ." Jenny hesitates, trying to find the right words to say. "I know you want to keep improving this team, and she is talented . . . And maybe my opinion doesn't hold that much weight since I won't be here next year . . . But, Coach, she's toxic."

Nods of affirmation reverberate throughout the circle.

"First of all, Jenny, your opinion does matter to me. And second, I do want to keep improving this team, which is why I said I didn't want her."

"Wait, for real?"

"Yup. Back when I asked you about her in our mid-season meetings, you were right, Jenny. She's a great lacrosse player, but a terrible person. I just wanted to let you know that she might be a little more . . . terrible this time around since she knows I turned her down."

"Good," Luna shoots back with a look of determination. "I like a challenge."

"Any changes we should make at midfield?" Rachel asks.

"Nope, just quick passes and possess the ball. That's the plan," Jason replies. "Oh, and maybe show off that new trademark on-the-run shot you've perfected."

The team begins to chant Rachel's name, imitating the crowd's reaction at the Johnson & Bellevue game.

"Ra-chel."

"Raa-chel!"

"Raaa-chel!"

"Oh, stop it," Rachel says, her cheeks blushing, and the chant slowly dies down.

"Wait . . . Why'd you stop?" she jokes, and laughter rings out amongst the team.

"Also, I know we like to call our defense *The Brick Wall*, but after our semifinal game, I think we might actually have a brick wall in goal," Luna adds, shooting Chloe a wink as she does. Chloe smiles, but doesn't look away.

"Very true, and, Chloe, I can't say enough how proud we all are of that performance. So, keep it up!" Jason boasts.

"Yeah, props, Chloe!" Rachel adds. "You crushed it."

A rush of agreement surges throughout the team.

"Get it, Chloe!"

"You da bomb!"

"She's the G.O.A.T in GOAL!"

"Ladies, truthfully, I don't have much more to say. There's no doubt tomorrow will be a challenge, but we've faced an onslaught of adversity so far this season, so I've got faith in us. Just make sure you get plenty of rest tonight, and tomorrow . . . show up ready to play. Jenny, break 'em down—"

"Wait, Coach," Jenny interrupts, "before we end practice, I want to mention that we're going to have a team dinner tonight at Sam's place. Do you want to come?"

Jason's heart skips a beat at the request.

"Coach . . .?" Jenny prompts.

"Yes, Jenny, I would love to come."

"Amazing! We aren't sure exactly what we're doing for food yet, but—"

"Wait, shit," Jason interjects. "I have an appointment at five o'clock tonight . . ."

"Okay, what if we moved it earlier and did . . . like a team lunch?"

"Seriously? You'd do that for me?"

"Hell yeah, Coach. You gotta be there. But what should we do for food?"

Jason can barely hold in his emotions as the team throws out suggestions, but then suddenly, a thought pops into his head. He reaches into his pocket and pulls out a matte black business card with the words *The Iron Penn* printed neatly in the center.

"Ladies, I think I have an idea."

CHAPTER 27

"Pass the fries!" Dahlia shouts out above the cacophony of voices bouncing throughout the luxury lounge inside The Iron Penn.

Jason is seated at the head of a large marble table that must be at least twenty feet long, with his players lining each side. Sprawled throughout the table is a wide variety of pub food: towering piles of nachos covered in a viscous yellow cheese, maple glazed barbeque wings, burgers with perfectly sculpted sesame seed buns, and crinkle cut garlic fries with an aroma that makes his mouth water.

"I'll pass the fries when you stop bogarting those wings!" Daisy yells back, then holds up a basket of the fries to offer a trade.

"Coach, this place is incredible. How'd you find out about it?" Rachel asks.

"Well—"

"Good afternoon, everyone!" Lucy announces to the room as she walks in with a large black tray covered in even more appetizers. "I've got the jalapeño poppers, the onion rings, and also a wonderful assortment of aiolis created from a supersecret family recipe that only three other people in the world know about!"

His players' eyes grow wide, and Lucy leans in toward Jason.

"I got them at the local supermarket," she whispers in his ear, then puts her finger to her lips. "Shhh . . ."

She gives him a wink as she turns and leaves the room.

Jason chuckles, then looks back at Rachel to answer her previous question. She has a wry smile plastered on her face. Jason raises an eyebrow, but then he quickly notices Jenny and Sam also share a similar expression.

"Soooooo . . ." Rachel says with a grin. "Who was that?"

"That was Lucy," Jason responds, knowing exactly where she's going with this.

"She's cute!" she replies, her face beaming, and Jason drops his head with mild embarrassment.

"It's not like that . . . We met when I first got here. Over the last few months, I've gotten to know her better, but she's just a friend. She's only being this polite because I'm renting out this room."

"Coach . . . I know chemistry when I see it, and you two . . . You've got it," Jenny adds.

"Oh, stop it."

"I'm serious! You've got a connection. I can feel it."

Lucy walks back into the room. "So, can I refresh anyone's drinks, or would anyone like to place an order for something else?"

"Yeah, I'll take a double-whiskey soda, light ice," Sam says confidently.

"The fuck you will," Jason replies in astonishment, leading Lucy to burst out laughing and have to turn away to hide her face.

Jenny and Rachel look at Jason and lift their eyebrows, as if to say, "See . . . we told you. She's into you."

Jason just shakes his head.

"Could we just get some more water for the table?"

"Sure thing," Lucy replies, then heads back toward the bar, still giggling.

Sam looks over at Jason just as she leaves the room. "Oh yeah. She wants you bad."

"Sam, please, no she does not."

"You know something, Coach: Denial isn't a good look on you."

"Sure, whatever you say . . . Also, a double-whiskey? At a team event?"

"What? Can't blame a girl for trying, right?"

"Fair enough." Jason sighs and looks down at his watch. Seeing the time, he pushes his chair back and goes to stand. The chair makes a loud *screech* across the floor, and the team looks in his direction.

As he gazes upon the girls, he clears his throat to speak. "Ladies, I don't know what tomorrow will bring, so I wanted to say a few things now before I have to head out to my appointment."

"Speeeeech!" Taya shouts from the far end of the table.

"Yes, Taya, speech time. Listen . . . When I got here, I didn't know what to expect. I was in a new place, coaching a new team; your head coach left us without saying a word, and I was truly . . . *truly* terrified." Jason stops to take a breath, remembering the challenges he's faced along the way. "I know we had our differences at the start—"

"You got that right . . . *Sam*," Taya says, shooting Sam a facetious look.

"Yeah, didn't you call him a bitch at our first practice?" Daisy adds.

"Yeah . . . Sorry about that," Sam replies, holding her hands up in contrition.

"Ladies, let him finish," Jenny states, taking control.

"As I was saying, I know we had our differences, but looking back now . . . I'd do it all again. When big changes occur, there will always be friction, but all I ever wanted to do was make a difference . . . And I really hope I did."

For a short while, no one in the room speaks. He sees Chloe wipe away a tear, then look at Luna. "You made a difference, Coach," she says with a smile.

"You really did," Rachel chimes in.

Jason's eyes well up from the overwhelming emotion that's enveloped him. Sam stands and raises her glass.

"You taught me never to judge a book by its cover, because, even though I'm currently raising a glass of water and *not* whiskey"—she uses her other hand to gesture toward her glass— "which I maintain is bullshit. You're not such a bad guy after all, and you're a damn good coach."

The rest of the team members stand, raising their glasses as well. Jason does the same, then uses his shirtsleeve to wipe a tear that has made its way down his cheek.

"Thank you," he replies with a sniffle. "Here's to you all, the best team a coach could ever ask for."

"Here, here," Jenny replies.

"Here, here," the table echoes.

Everyone clinks their glasses, takes a sip, and then returns to their seats.

Clap, clap, clap, clap, clap. The sound is coming from the doorway behind Jason, and he turns to see Lucy standing on the threshold.

"That was fucking beautiful."

Sam leans in toward Jason and whispers, "Oh, she's got a mouth on her, too. I like her."

Jason rolls his eyes and turns to Lucy. "Thank you, Lucy." Then he raises his glass back up into the air. "And here's to Lucy! An amazing host and wonderful person."

"Here, here," the girls say in unison, and she turns to leave.

"Wait, Lucy!" Jenny calls out.

"Yes?"

"Are you coming to our championship game tomorrow?"

"Am I coming to your championship game tomorrow?" Lucy looks out upon the table of wide, unblinking eyes, then looks at Jason. "I wouldn't miss it for the world."

"Amazing!" Jenny cheers, as she and Sam both shoot another glance over at Jason.

"Can't wait to see you there," he replies with a smile.

After she leaves, the rest of the girls have the same expressions and playful grins that Jenny and Sam have.

"Ladies, stop. We're just friends."

"Suuuure you are," Taya snickers from the other end of the table, leading to even more laughter.

Jason joins in before quickly glancing at his watch to check the time. "Shoot. Ladies, I have to go, but I will see you tomorrow at 10 a.m. Rest up and come ready to play!"

As he goes to leave, Sam quickly follows and grabs his arm to stop him.

Out of earshot from the others, she asks, "Coach, what's this appointment you're going to?"

Jason looks down at the floor, then back at Sam. "I decided to finally take the advice of people who care about me."

Her brow furrows in confusion until she realizes what he's talking about. "Oh . . . Well, I'm proud of you for taking this step to better yourself."

"Thank you . . . Honestly, I'm still a little nervous."

"Coach, to quote a very wise man, sometimes . . . you just gotta take the leap."

Jason grins as he fondly remembers the words he said to her only a few weeks ago.

"Thank you, Captain, you're right . . . It's time to take the leap."

CHAPTER 28

Causality. Jason had heard this word before from a teacher back in high school. He can remember her saying, *"It's the idea that one event or decision leads to another, and then another. The cause of one decision leads to the effect of another."*

At the time, Jason hadn't really paid much attention to the meaning of the word. He just enjoyed the way the syllables rolled off his tongue when he said it. But now, as he sits on a floral-patterned chair in a dimly lit waiting room, *causality* is the only thing on his mind. *How did I end up here?*

Jason's mind wanders back to that fateful summer after his first year in college. He was only nineteen years old and had barely survived his first year at Syracuse. He managed to skate by with a C-average GPA, which, as he thinks back, was an absolute miracle considering the state he was in.

Jason had instigated all three of the fights that eventually led to his being kicked off the lacrosse team before the spring season had even started. The fights were meaningless. He wasn't goaded into them. He was just angry and in pain, and he wanted to hurt someone. Looking back, he deeply regrets getting into these altercations—the people he tried to fight didn't even want to be involved. They were just in the wrong place at the wrong time when Jason lost control. The only solace Jason still takes from these fights is that he was so drunk, he barely got a good shot in—he basically just got his ass kicked by innocent bystanders doing nothing more than defending themselves.

Thankfully for him, none of the victims pressed charges, but the resulting hearings in front of the school board were daunting enough. The topic of all these hearings was simple—*Should Jason Nash be allowed to remain in school, or should he be expelled for his actions?*

The days that followed were dreadful. Jason would show up to a stuffy room early in the morning, dressed in an ill-fitting suit, and sit in front of a panel of individuals who made up the school board. They would ask him questions regarding the incidents and listen closely as he did his best to defend his actions. Jason had the option to call in anyone who would be willing to speak to his character—which, at the time, was a very short list. With every day that passed, Jason was convinced that his time in college was over until, out of nowhere, Chuck Garcia showed up. Jason hadn't spoken to him since graduating high school, but he had sent him an email on a whim, hoping that he might show up. To this day, Jason still remembers everything Chuck said as he spoke calmly into the microphone, defending Jason's future:

> Ladies and gentlemen of the School Board, today, I would like to speak about the past. I recognize full well that the actions of Jason Nash were unjust and reprehensible, but these were not the actions of a man acting with malice; these were the actions of a man in need of help. He lost his twin sister in a car accident a year ago, and after one parent abandoned him, and the other was unwilling to help, he came out to college with no lifelines and a suitcase full of pain.
>
> Can any of you say you know what that's like? Can any of you admit to knowing the stress this could put on a person? College is hard enough to navigate as you try to discover the person you want to become, all while trying to find a new community in a new and unfamiliar place. This man was asked to do all this after he lost his entire world.
>
> So I ask you, look into your hearts and see the good still left in this man. Show him the compassion and care that life never did. Don't fault him for his past . . . Give him the chance to embrace his future, and prove to the world that he has the capacity to change.

Every time Jason thinks back to Chuck's testimony, he remembers the emotion that flooded into his body. He was sure the world had given up on him, and his life was over. Nevertheless, here was a man who was willing to put his reputation on the line to fight for his future. This was the moment that Jason decided he wanted to help people. Soon after, he was allowed to stay in school, and Chuck made sure to call him a few times a week to make sure he was okay. This was the start of a bond that would ensure Jason crossed the finish line. Without Chuck, Jason never would've made it to graduation. *Causality.*

When Jason graduated at twenty-two, he was still very much unsure of his future. He knew he wanted to help people, but beyond that, it was a mystery. Depression would set in on lonely nights when Jason felt overwhelmed by the sheer length of life and the idea of never discovering his true passion. *What if I'm lying on my deathbed, and after eighty years of life, I realize that I never truly lived?*

When those thoughts popped into his head, it was Chuck who would talk him off the ledge. It didn't matter if it was six o'clock in the morning, or eleven o'clock at night; if Jason called, Chuck would answer.

After a few years of trying different jobs and considering different career paths, Chuck came up with a plan.

"You want to help people; you want to do something that keeps you active and engaged, and you still love lacrosse. So, why not try coaching?"

Jason mulled over the idea for a few days before he decided it was something worth trying—and about one year later, Jason finally secured his first official coaching job as a varsity high school boys lacrosse coach. If Jason hadn't made it to graduation, his choices for a career path would've been limited, and he never would've found coaching. *Causality.*

Four years later, after developing the players within his program and honing his own coaching skills to the best of his ability, the voice of Chuck still rattled around in his brain: *"Move or rust."* This simple thought is what led Jason to search for a collegiate coaching job to further his career path within the coaching field.

After months of searching and wondering if he'd ever get the opportunity to coach at the collegiate level, the phone call came in from the Crystal Summit recruiter. If Jason hadn't found coaching as a career path, he never would've received this phone call. *Causality.*

He can still recall the feeling of utter terror and gloom that would bubble up anytime a new challenge came his way after he accepted the job and relocated his whole life to Pittsburgh, Pennsylvania—and the challenges never seemed to stop. First, there was the team's original uncertainty as he arrived and Sam's outright disdain toward him. And the head coach quit on Jason's first day, abandoning the team. Plus, he experienced a multitude of panic attacks throughout the season. And if all that wasn't bad enough, he'd had a hostile interaction with a fan that led to a three-game suspension.

Any of these challenges could have sent him over the edge and made him decide to give up—but he didn't. Even when the present looked bleak and the future looked downright terrifying, Jason kept moving forward. Had Jason not received the call to coach at Crystal Summit, he never would've been tested like this, which means he never would've had the opportunity to open up to his team and eventually win them over. *Causality.*

Finally, there were the events that led him here. Jason opened up to his team about his past, just like Chuck had said he should. He let them in, and their relationship grew stronger because of it. After that, he had a meltdown that led to Sam and him having an unbelievably constructive conversation about their past, and how to deal with trauma. He can still hear her saying, *"Your past doesn't dictate your future."* Because of his conversation with Sam, he found the strength to keep moving forward. Tomorrow, he will lead his team into a championship game, but today, he's here, contemplating causality.

Without Chuck, Jason never would've graduated. Had Jason

not graduated, he never would've found coaching. If he'd never found coaching, he never would've been offered the job at Crystal Summit. Had they not offered him the job, he never would've opened up to his team about his past. If he hadn't opened up to his team, he wouldn't have had that conversation with Sam. And without that conversation with Sam, he never would've ended up here.

But Chuck *did* help him graduate, and now he's *here*, sitting in *this* dimly lit room, on *this* floral-patterned chair, waiting for the office door in front of him to open, and have his name called.

It's amazing how one small, seemingly insignificant decision you make can have such a profound impact on your life or somebody else's. *Causality.*

The door in front of Jason swings open, and Dr. Jennifer Parsons walks out.

"Hello, Jason; come on in."

CHAPTER 29

The drive to the field house feels different this morning. The world around Jason seems more inviting, and the colors more vibrant. Even the sun seems to shine brighter as its heat radiates down to Earth. He has his window down to feel the cool breeze blow past him, and the air smells fresher than it ever has before. Today is the biggest game of his coaching career, but Jason isn't nervous. *Is this what being relaxed feels like? Maybe Chuck was onto something with this whole therapy thing.*

When Jason pulls into the parking lot, Sam is just getting out of her car. He can see she has headphones on and can't hear him approaching. He creeps his car up behind her and then lays on his horn with a loud *honk!*

"Fuck!" she screams out, leaping backward in fear.

Jason can't contain his laughter, and Sam flips him the bird as he puts the car into park and exits the vehicle.

"I deserve that." He chuckles as she lowers her finger and walks toward him.

"You scared the shit out of me!"

"I know, I know, I'm sorry. I couldn't help myself."

As Sam approaches Jason, she looks at him with a peculiar expression.

"You seem different."

"Different how?"

"I don't know . . . Just, different," she says. "You look good, Coach."

"Well, thank you. I feel good. Like, really good."

"I'm guessing this means your session went well?"

"I already have another one scheduled for next week. It was genuinely amazing."

"So, you took the leap?"

"Yes, I did, and I came out the other side okay. It seems so silly now, thinking about how afraid I was before."

"Well, I'm happy for you. Now, are you ready to head inside? Or do you want to scare the shit out of anyone else while you're out here?"

"Let's head inside," he says, clearly amused.

As they turn to walk toward the field house, Jason stops dead in his tracks when he sees the figure standing at the front door. An older man, close to six feet tall, with graying hair and a thin stubble beard, is standing right beneath the archway leading inside.

"Coach, are you okay?" Sam asks.

Jason doesn't answer. After a few seconds pass, his look of shock morphs into one of pure elation.

"Chuck!" Jason screams out, and he takes off running toward the door at full speed. When he arrives, he vaults into his arms and embraces him with a hug. "I can't believe you came!"

"Are you kidding me? I wouldn't miss your championship game! This is a huge accomplishment!"

Sam approaches from behind, and Chuck looks over at her. "And who might you be, young lady?"

"Hello, sir, I'm Sam."

"Well, nice to meet you, Sam, and you can call me Chuck."

"Nice to meet you, too, Chuck."

"Are you excited for today's game?"

"Incredibly excited, but I'm also kind of nervous. This may be the last collegiate lacrosse game I ever play."

"Well, I've been watching you this season, and I think you're going to do amazing. And as for what comes next, I can tell just from meeting you now, your future is bright."

"Wow, thank you, Chuck. Now I see where Coach gets his positive attitude."

"Ha! I'm flattered, Sam. I did teach this man everything he knows."

"So modest, Chuck," Jason replies with a laugh.

"Well, I've got to go get ready, but it was very nice meeting you," Sam says to Chuck.

"You as well! And good luck out there today. I know you're going to do great."

She heads inside, leaving Jason and Chuck to talk.

"So, how are you feeling, Jason?"

"Really good. Actually, I have something to tell you."

"What's that?"

"I um . . . I went to therapy yesterday."

Chuck's eyes grow wide and immediately well up. Without warning, he grabs Jason and pulls him in for a hug.

"That's incredible. I'm so proud of you, Jason."

Chuck goes to pull away, but Jason doesn't let go. This is the closest he's felt to Chuck in a long time, both physically and emotionally. He hasn't seen him in months, and he doesn't want this moment to end.

"This really is a huge step, Jason. You've come a long way in the last few months."

"I'm so happy you're here, Chuck."

"Me too, Jason. Me too. Now, go in there and get your team pumped up for this game. I'll be watching from the stands."

Jason starts to walk away, but Chuck stops him. "Oh, wait, Jason, I almost forgot! I have something for you." Chuck holds out a small black box.

"What is it?"

"Open it."

Jason removes the lid. At first, he's not sure what it is, but after a few seconds, he slowly starts to understand and puts his hand to his face as tears well up in his eyes.

"For your lapel. I think it'll add a bit of color to this moratorium look you've got going on," Chuck adds, gesturing toward Jason's all-black suit.

"Chuck . . . this is amazing. Thank you."

"You're about to coach a collegiate championship lacrosse game," Chuck responds. "She should be with you."

Jason places the lid back on the box and looks at Chuck. "I have so much I want to say."

"We'll have plenty of time to talk after. I'll see you out there," Chuck replies before putting a hand on Jason's shoulder and looking him in the eyes. "Never stop."

"Never stop," Jason says, then heads inside to join the team.

***

"Ladies, I want to say a few things before Coach arrives," Sam announces to the locker room.

The players are seated in their respective lockers, getting locked in for the game—those wearing headphones remove them and turn their attention toward Sam.

"This has been a long, arduous fucking season, and if you had told me when Coach Nash showed up that we'd all be sitting here right now, prepping for this championship game . . . I'd have said you were fucking nuts. We've come a long way, and this may be my final game as a Blue Jay . . . So, I just wanted to say how incredible this ride has been." Sam looks away as her face starts to tremble. "Sorry, I know I'm not someone who typically gets emotional."

"Geez, Coach has really turned you into a big softy," Jenny says with a smile.

"I know. His positivity is like a fucking disease," she replies, generating laughter from the room.

"Well, I'll echo what Sam just said," Jenny adds. "The truth is . . . I don't know who I'd be today if I hadn't come here to play lacrosse—and when we finally leave this place . . . I won't remember the scores, or any mistakes we might've made along the way. I'll just remember the laughs we all shared, the inside jokes, the late nights and early mornings . . . I'll remember the time we spent together, and how lucky I was to share it with all of you."

Muffled sniffles can be heard throughout the room as the emotional truth of the situation sets in. For the seniors, this could be the last game they ever play. For everyone else, this could be the last chance they get to play with their seniors.

"Fuuuuck!" Rachel screams out, beginning to tear up as she runs over to share a hug with her seniors. "I'm really going to miss you guys."

The players around the room all follow suit and embrace each other, forming a group hug and creating a massive sea of powder blue as they come together.

When the circle eventually subsides, Sam adds, "You know, Rachel, I'm really liking this side of you that's okay with cursing."

"Well, someone's gotta pick up the slack after you're gone."

While the team giggles together at Rachel's comment, the door swings open.

***

"Shit, what did I miss! This looks like one hell of a moment."

The team slowly separates and returns to their lockers.

"We were just discussing how this could be our last game, and how happy we are to have shared it with each other," Jenny responds.

"Well, that's beautiful," Jason replies, "but let's not call it yet. After all, a win today gets us a bid into the NCAA D1 Tournament."

The team nods in agreement, and as they do, Chloe leans forward and squints while she inspects Jason's lapel.

"Coach, is that a wat—?"

"Water lily. Yes, it is. My mentor just gave me this. He said a little piece of my sister should be with us on the sideline today."

"Goddammit, Coach . . . Now *that* is beautiful," Jenny chimes in.

"Thank you. Now let's get down to business," Jason replies, then walks to the center of the room. "I know there isn't a soul in this room who's been here before. This is Crystal Summit's first winning season in five years, so this may feel like your biggest test yet . . . But it's not."

The players look around the room at one another, clearly perplexed, but no one questions the statement.

"I'm not saying this is going to be easy," Jason continues, "but this season alone has brought more challenge and adversity into your lives than a single game ever could. And yet, you are all still standing. So today . . . Today is just another game. Before the very first game I coached here, I told you that there were no more good teams or bad teams, but simply teams standing in our way. And, ladies . . . on our path to that trophy, there is only one team that remains. So get up, go out there, and show them who you are!"

"Yeah!"

"Let's go!"

"Ain't no one better than us!"

As the chants ring out, Jason opens the door to the locker room, and the team floods out like a river through a broken dam. Their energy is incredible, their passion is flowing, and their spirit is undeniable.

We got this shit, he thinks, and they storm out onto the field, like a pack of lions ready for the hunt.

***

The first half of the game flew by faster than Jason expected. He was always told that big events can sometimes seem to elapse quicker, because your mind is so involved that you seldom have time to stop and think. But as the halftime whistle sounds, he gets a minute of peace—or better yet, ten minutes of peace—to reflect on the first half and make any adjustments needed. While Emerald Hills heads to the locker room, Jason decides to keep his team out on the field to save as much time as possible, and with the way the first half went, he'll need every second.

The scoreboard reads 8–9, with Emerald Hills in the lead. Both teams have been playing at an extremely high caliber, and Jason can't help but take a minute to appreciate the fact that these games—games where both teams are fighting for every inch and playing their absolute hearts out—are the games that make coaching worthwhile.

With the girls huddling up around him, and water bottles being passed around the circle, he takes a breath before speaking. "First off, great fucking work out there. We knew it wasn't going to be easy, but you all are holding your own against the highest echelon of players."

"Hell yeah!" Maddy shouts.

"Woo, woo!" Nicole hollers.

"Luna, exceptional work shutting down Juliana so far. She's only taken"—Jason looks down at his halftime stat sheet that was handed to him only moments ago—"three shots on goal so far, and our rockstar goalie, Chloe, has saved every last one!"

"She's a beast in net!" Sam exclaims.

"Indeed, she is. Now, let's get to the adjustments. They're clearly trying to shut down Maddy and Nicole, similar to the game against Johnson & Bellevue when Rachel made that *killer* on-the-run goal to seal the game."

"Rachel the sniper!" Taya yells out.

"Yes. That shot was amazing, but my point is, she had the opening because our twins were being locked off. So, to all my midfielders, if you see a clear and open path to the cage, take it. Sound good?"

The midfielders yell out an array of responses.

"No doubt, Coach."

"Hell yeah."

"Goals on goals on goals."

Jason's gaze shifts to the scoreboard. *Just under two minutes of halftime remaining.*

"Alright, I love that your spirits are still high, because we're going to need every ounce of talent for this second half. This is not the time for complacency. This is not the time for apathy. This is the time for pure, unbridled fucking effort." Jason looks around the circle of players, scanning their faces. "We are one team, and we have one dream. Got it? One team, one dream. One team, one dream. One team—"

"One dream!" the entire team screams out.

"One team!" Jason continues.

"One dream!"

"One team!"

"One dream!"

"Let's do this!" Jason hollers, raising his arms to the sky, causing an uproar of screams around him.

The halftime buzzer sounds. Emerald Hills emerges from the locker room. Both teams take the field, and the second half begins.

Only minutes into the second half, the Blue Jays strike first with an exceptional fast break goal scored by Nicole, who was able to break free from her defender and pin the top-right corner of the cage.

"We got this," Jason says to himself, watching from the sideline.

The stadium is loud with cheers as the team celebrates their goal, but then, a voice cuts through the commotion.

"Coach! Coach! Rachel's down!" Dahlia is yelling at him from the sideline and pointing toward Rachel, who has collapsed to the turf and is gripping her ankle as the athletic trainer rushes onto the field toward her.

Jason looks at Dahlia. "What happened?" he asks, assuming she must've taken an awkward step and rolled her ankle.

"It was number 15," Dahlia replies abruptly, gesturing toward an Emerald Hills player who has quickly exited the field. "She tripped her."

"What? Are you certain?"

"I'm positive, Coach. I saw the whole thing."

Jason freezes. A sharp pang of tinnitus rattles in his eardrums. His heart starts pounding in his chest. He can feel his adrenaline spike as his face goes pale and his mind goes red. He turns his attention to the Emerald Hills coach.

"Hey! Hey, you!" he screams out, angrily thrusting his finger toward the coach. "Is this what you teach your players? Huh?! Take out the opposing team's talent just to try and win?!"

Jason's feet have taken over as he quickly closes the distance between them. His anger quickly boils over, making his heart race.

"Hey! I'm talking to you!" he screams out again, seeing the coach desperately trying to avoid his gaze.

Jason can feel he's losing control, but before he can go any further, a voice rings out to his right.

"Coach, stop!"

Sam has now run off the field and thrown herself in front of him.

"Coach. You have to stop. It's not worth it."

Jason looks at her with fury in his eyes. He fights the urge to keep going, as his body wants so badly to give in to the rage that flows through it.

"Coach, if not for me . . . do it for her." Sam points to his lapel. "Do it for Lilly."

Within seconds, his head starts to center, and the fog clears from his mind. He glances down at the flower, then back up at Sam. Without a word, he gives her a nod, and there's an unspoken moment of understanding between them. She gives him a nod back, then returns to the field.

Jason's breathing is still heavy and labored as Rachel is helped to the sideline.

He looks at the trainer. "Will she be okay?"

"Yes, just a sprain, but she's out for the rest of the game."

"Fuck," he spits out under his breath, then looks toward the sideline. "Alright, Dahlia, you're going in. And, Dahlia"—he leans in close—"make them fucking pay for this."

He can see sparks of ferocity flash in her eyes, and a frightening grin forms on her face.

"Yes, Coach," she replies, then walks out onto the field.

***

Fweet! Fweet!

The whistle sounds to end the third quarter, and Jason's squad has bounced back with a vengeance. Dahlia clearly took his "Make them fucking pay" comment to heart, as she managed to score three goals within a very short time. Emerald Hills, however, is not letting up. They responded well with a few goals of their own, making the score 17–15 as they head into the fourth quarter, with Crystal Summit in the lead. Both teams switch sides, and the final quarter begins.

Jason's heartbeat is like a jackhammer as the minutes tick away. The game is happening so quickly he can't seem to focus or maintain a grasp on what is going on around him. It's like a tennis match of back-and-forth goal scoring. Emerald Hills goal, Crystal Summit goal, Emerald Hills goal, Crystal Summit goal. The pattern goes on and on in what very well may be the highest-scoring game Jason has ever coached. Defense has gone out the window, and it's simply a question of whose offense will strike the hardest before time expires and the final whistle sounds.

In what feels like the blink of an eye, Jason looks at the scoreboard, and only 45 seconds remain. It's a dead heat with the score tied at 24.

How the fuck did we get here?

Crystal Summit's offense maintains possession but is struggling to penetrate. Nicole has the ball down low, but the defense for Emerald Hills is in an all-out press, locking off every player on the field. Jason can see the writing on the wall . . . He's been here before . . . The opponent is playing all-out defense, and Nicole is exhausted with no one to pass to. It's only a matter of time before she loses the ball, and Emerald Hills takes off in the other direction.

Jenny is up top and being pushed back further away from the action. She keeps taking steps backward toward the restraining line, and as Jason watches, his chest tightens. His ears start ringing, and his vision blurs.

No, no, no. Not now. This can't happen now.

He closes his eyes and drops his head as his legs turn to jelly, and the panic envelops him.

So this is how it ends . . .

When all hope seems lost, and nothing but dread remains, he hears it.

"Northwestern!"

Jason's eyes shoot open, and his mind comes to. As he lifts his head, time seems to slow to a crawl. *Did I hear that right? Am I imagining things?*

"Northwestern!"

He hears it again, and this time, he can see Sam shouting the word from her defensive end. Jason's gaze shifts to Jenny as she takes two steps backward and hops over the thirty-yard restraining line. Afterwards, Jason's eyes shift to Sam. Right on cue, as Jenny crosses the line, she takes off running.

For years to come, Jason will recall what happens next to be the single greatest thing to ever occur in collegiate sports history.

Sure, many people will say it was just another trick play, but to him, this wasn't just about lacrosse; this wasn't just a play . . . this was everything.

The way Sam sprints toward the cage looks elegant and majestic as the other team yells at each other, desperately trying to figure out what to do. Nicole sees Sam barreling down the field and whips the ball her way, hitting her in stride. It is utter mayhem for the defense, as no one knows who is supposed to slide and pick her up, so Sam runs uncontested toward the net, then effortlessly bounces the ball between the goalie's legs. It all happens so fast, and then, shortly after, the final whistle sounds.

Fweet! Fweet! Fweeeeeeeet!

Every player on the sideline looks around in shock, as if needing confirmation that what just happened truly did happen, and wasn't just a figment of their imagination. The reality sets in, and all at once, they storm the field.

"Let's *fucking* goooooo!"

The words pour out of Jason's mouth without control. His hair stands on end as goosebumps cover his body. Elation rushes through his veins, and a smile forms on his face that he feels may never leave. Jason looks around in awe at the pandemonium taking place around him. His team is celebrating, and the fans in the stands are going ballistic. As he scans the stadium, he sees Chuck looking down at him. Though he's about a hundred feet away, he's fairly certain, as they lock eyes, he can see him mouth the words, "You did it."

Before Jason looks away, he spots a tall woman with jet-black hair, raising a giant powder blue foam finger into the air as she cheers. "Lucy," he says with a smile, "she made it."

His team sprints over, and he looks at them with pride and fulfillment in his eyes.

"Ladies . . ." His eyes immediately fill with tears as he gets choked up. "I have so much I want to say . . . Today, you accomplished something incredible. When the stakes were at their highest, you didn't panic; you didn't overthink it. You simply went out there and played lacrosse. And . . ." His throat swells, and tears start flowing down his cheeks. "You brought Lilly's and my play to life . . . I love you all." Jason stops, unable to keep speaking, and Jenny firmly places her hand on his shoulder.

"Couldn't have done it without you. Never give up, right?"

"Damn right, Jenny . . . Damn right."

"Make way; make way," a voice calls out from outside the huddle, and a path forms.

As the circle opens, Bill walks in holding a large bronze trophy. There are many words inscribed on it, but Jason's mind seems to block them all out and fixate on only one. As he stares at the word lying dead center in the middle of the brass plate, the smile on his face grows even bigger.

Champions.

Jason looks at Jenny and Sam. "Think you could give me a hand lifting this thing?"

"I didn't know it until now, but I've been waiting all season to hear you say those words," Sam replies.

"A-fucking-men," Jenny affirms.

All three of them reach down and grip the trophy. Their fingers wrap around the heavy metal base, and they lift it toward the sapphire-blue sky. The yellow sun glints off the shimmering trophy, and Jason shouts enthusiastically, "We're going to the NCAA Division 1 Tournament!"

As they hoist the trophy above their heads, the entire team stands around them, screaming so loud in excitement that he can't even hear himself think, but he doesn't care. Because at that moment, everything is right with the world.

Chapter 30

"Ahem, is this thing on?" Jason taps the microphone in front of him, and it responds with a loud *screech*.

Jason gazes out at the seated crowd in front of him. His entire team, along with their families, are scattered throughout the room while he stands behind a tall oak podium at the front of the ballroom. The lights are brighter than he would've liked, but as he adjusts the tie that's tightly knotted up in a double Windsor around his neck, he actually feels quite relaxed.

"Ladies and gentlemen, thank you all for coming. Today, as we all feast at this post-season banquet, I'd like to take some time to say a few words regarding what I believe to be the single greatest season in this school's history, and by far and away the most influential and talented team I've ever had the pleasure of coaching."

"Blue Jays fuh life!" Taya shouts from the crowd.

"Damn right, Taya," he responds. "The truth is, when I first came to this school . . . I was afraid. Afraid of making such a big change in my life, afraid of being in a new place, and quite honestly . . . afraid of being alone. But as I look at you all now . . ." Jason's eyes scan the faces of everyone seated in front of him, listening intently, and hanging on every word he's saying. Pride surges through him as he presses on. "As I look at you all now, I feel an incredible warmth knowing that . . . I'm not alone anymore. We all faced challenges throughout this season. Some of you didn't enjoy my presence at first, but over time, we eventually started to see eye to eye."

Cough, cough. "Sam." *Cough, cough.* Maddy's fake coughs make the crowd laugh, giving Jason a chance to stop and breathe before continuing.

"Yes, we had our differences . . . But after a while, we realized that we had quite a bit in common as well."

Sam looks toward Jason, at his spot behind the podium, and gives him a long nod in agreement.

"The truth is, all I ever wanted to do was make a difference. Yes, I've said this before, but I really do mean it. I know I'm not perfect. Hell, Prescott Ridge definitely knows I'm not perfect."

"We got your back, Coach!" a parent yells out. "That guy was a dick!"

Another wave of laughter rolls through the crowd.

"I appreciate that, sir. I guess what I want to say is that I'm extremely proud of you all, and I wish I had said it more during the season. Every one of you has tackled some kind of adversity this year. Some of you conquered the fear of failure." Jason looks at Rachel with a smile. "Some of you conquered the fear of risk and change." Jason looks at Jenny with a smile. "And some of you conquered the fear of the great unknown by taking a leap of faith and hoping not to get hurt on the other side." Jason looks at Chloe. He sees her father sitting to her right, but there is a woman sitting to her left as well, with her arm around her shoulder.

She finally came.

"You all conquered those challenges with confidence, and although we ended up losing in the first round of the NCAA tournament, you all still have so much to be proud of."

"You got that right!" Maddy yells out.

"Yeah, we put the entire NCAA on notice!" Nicole shouts.

"You're damn right we did," Jason agrees. "I know we have a few seniors leaving us this season, and to all of you, I hope your futures are bright and full of love, happiness, and success."

"Here, here!" Jenny's dad yells out, raising a glass.

"Here, here!" the crowd says in unison.

Jason lifts his glass as well, then takes a sip before placing it back down on the podium.

"To everyone else . . . well, I don't know if you know this, but when I came here, I was only hired to finish out this season . . . This morning, however, I signed a three-year extension . . . so we'll be back next year!"

The players look at each other and start murmuring excitedly.

"Oh, fuck yeah."

"We're going for it *all* next year."

"Let's goooo."

"I just want to say one final thing before I finish. As I've said, this job has had many ups and downs along the way. It's been hard, stressful, and even downright painful at times . . . But this job also changed my life. It gave me the opportunity of a lifetime; it gave me a family I'll cherish forever, and it gave me memories I'll never forget. So, even with all the hardship that came along the way, if I were given the chance to go back, I'd do it all again. Taking this job . . . Best decision I ever made, because it led me to all of you."

The crowd applauds as Jason leaves the podium. His eyes well up with tears of happiness as he makes his way back to his seat. This is his new home. This is his new family. And now, as he looks around him, he knows with absolute certainty . . . he's not alone.

EPILOGUE

Jason looks down at the menu in front of him. It's been five months since the banquet, and he is now sitting in a small breakfast spot in Pittsburgh. A feeling of warmth runs through him as he reads the words "BAGELS BY JENNY" written across the top of the menu.

"Hey, Coach! Glad you could make it!" Jenny states happily as she approaches.

She's wearing a dark green uniform, with her tied up in a neat bun.

"This place is amazing," he replies, "and so full of customers! I can't believe you were able to open so quickly."

"Well, thankfully, I had saved up enough to put the down payment on the lease right after graduation. It really has been quite a trip these last few months! Do you want anything to eat or drink?"

"Can I get an iced coffee, please?"

"One iced coffee coming right up!" she replies. "Will Lucy be joining you today?"

"No, unfortunately, she got stuck at the bar, but she is very excited to see this place, so she'll be coming by soon enough."

"Lovely! Well, I'll go get you that iced coffee."

Vrr, vrr. Jason's phone vibrates on the table in front of him. Stealing a quick glance at the caller ID before he answers, he sees that it's Chuck calling him.

"Hey, Chuck!"

"Jason! How's life, buddy?"

"Really good. I'm actually at Jenny's new bagel spot I told you about. She's created a really nice place."

"That's great to hear! Well, I also wanted to call and see how therapy's been treating you. I know you said you've been going once a week."

"Yup, and it's going great. I was actually just about to try something Dr. Parsons suggested in our last meeting."

"Oh yeah? What's that?"

"Well, I told her how the past year of coaching was a fairly life-changing experience, so she suggested writing about it."

"Oh, wow, that sounds lovely. So, like, an autobiography of sorts?"

"Yeah, something like that. But honestly . . . I don't really know where to start. Any chance you could offer me some help?"

"Sorry, Jason, but I can't help you there."

"What? Why not? You've helped me every step along the way; why can't you help me now?"

"It's not that I *can't* help you, Jason. In fact, I'd really love to. But, Jason, this isn't my story . . . it's yours."

Jason sighs. "I suppose you're right."

"I always am," Chuck says with a smirk. "Shoot, I have to run, but it was nice talking to you, and good luck."

"Thanks, Chuck," he replies, then ends the call.

Jason pulls out a notebook from the bag on his left and uncaps his pen. "Alright . . . where to begin?" he says to himself.

Leaning back in his chair, he closes his eyes and clears his mind, thinking over what Chuck just said. *"This isn't my story . . . It's yours."*

Jason recalls the events that transpired over the last few months. The ups, the downs, the highs, and the lows. While his mind reflects, he gradually sits back up in his chair and opens his eyes. He takes the pen and presses it against the page, the blue ink slowly bleeding into the paper as he writes.

For the longest time, Jason Nash didn't have the slightest idea what he wanted to do with his life . . .

The End

Acknowledgements

First, I would like to acknowledge the incredible artists at 100covers for helping create an amazing cover for this novel. I'd also like to thank the ever-talented copyright editor Jen S. for her exceptional work in helping make sure this book was brought into the world in its most perfect form.

I would've never found coaching had I not played lacrosse as a kid, so, next I'd like to acknowledge two truly influential coaches from my past—Brian Hamm & Bucky Brandt. Thank you for everything you did to help mold me into the man I am today and thank you for giving me the tools I needed to become a leader of my own. I know I may have been a bittersweet combination of sarcasm and talent on the lacrosse field, but you always did your best to handle it with patience and grace—and on top of everything else, you never gave up on me, and for that I am eternally grateful.

Next, I would like to acknowledge every player I have ever coached. As I'm sure you saw at the beginning of this book, I dedicated it to all of you . . . And I did not make that dedication lightly. Each and every one of you has played such a meaningful role in my life, and I wouldn't trade the time we spent together for anything in the world. You've given my life fulfillment and meaning, and you helped me find my passion, while simultaneously giving me another family to love, admire, and care for. Without you, this book would've never been written . . . So, to all of you, thank you.

Finally, I would like to thank my twin brother, Christopher Walker. While coaching may have given me the educational and emotional experience to help write this book, my brother was truly the inspiration behind writing it. Since I came into this world only four minutes after he did, he has always been the person I turn to when I'm seeking guidance. He is my other half, he is my rock, and he will always be my best friend. So, thank you, Brother, for everything.

I'd like to give one final message to the world of coaching:

To the Coaches: Remember that it is not only our job, but it is our responsibility, to do everything we can to help our players become the very best they can be. No exceptions.

And to the Players: Remember that no matter how hard things get, you will always have the power to write your own story. No one can stop you from becoming the person you want to be, so long as *you* believe it is possible. So, in the face of even the toughest challenges . . . Never give up, never back down, and never stop.

Thank you for reading.

www.ingramcontent.com/pod-product-compliance
Lightning Source LLC
Chambersburg PA
CBHW020404110726
47899CB00006B/1858